Penny Kl............., psychologist
and stud........nor. She now writes full time,
and has written four books for adults – DYING TO
HELP, FEELING BAD, A CRUSHING BLOW and
TURNING NASTY. A WATERY GRAVE and
DEATHLY SILENCE – her first books for children
– are also published by Hodder Children's Books.

Penny Kline is married with two grown-up children,
and lives in Bath with her husband and her dog.

A Choice of Evils

Penny Kline

Hodder
Children's
Books

a division of Hodder Headline plc

A Catalogue record for this book is available from
the British Library

ISBN 0 340 66096 1

Typeset by Avon Dataset Ltd, Bidford-on-Avon

Printed and bound in Great Britain by
Cox & Wyman, Reading, Berks

Hodder Children's Books
A division of Hodder Headline plc
338 Euston Road
London NW1 3BH

One

Months later Karen would wake from a bad dream and wonder if she should have done something different. Told someone else? But what good would it have done? *Someone had got away with something really evil. Did it happen quite often?* Karen could remember how she and her father had discussed this very subject, ages ago when he was still living at home, but how could she have imagined that one day she herself would become involved with such a person.

The day it all began was boiling hot. Karen had wanted to go swimming but Laura persuaded her to go to a garden party at the home of some people called Tremlett who lived on the edge of the city, in the part where the houses had gardens that ran down to the river.

'Oh, come on Karen, it's not really a party, just some fund-raising thing. Anyway, I want you to meet Hannah.'

'Who's Hannah?' They were sitting on a wall outside Laura's house, watching the shimmering heat haze above the tarmac in Blenheim Road. When she left home, Karen's mother and Alex had been stretched out on their new reclining chairs, next to the soggy, smelly place that Alex called the Water Garden. Both were wearing skimpy sunbathing outfits. Neither had the figure for them.

'Hannah Tremlett,' said Laura, flicking back the lock of hair that kept falling over one eye.

Karen grinned. 'You've been doing that ever since you had it restyled. Doesn't it drive you crazy?'

'Look, d'you want to hear, or not?' said Laura impatiently. 'Mr and Mrs Tremlett, that's Hannah's grandparents, know my grandmother. No, hang on, let me finish. It's just the kind of story you love, except it's not a story and it only happened four months ago.'

'What did?' Karen was looking at her watch.

'At the end of April the Tremletts were staying at a house in North Devon. Masses of them. Grandparents, parents, aunts, uncles, they're that kind of family. Apparently Hannah and her parents were swimming in the sea and . . .' She paused, for greater effect. 'Hannah's mother got caught in a current, and drowned.'

'How old is this Hannah?'

'Eleven. No, twelve. But I haven't told you the worst bit. Hannah's father had to choose who to save.'

'His wife or his daughter.' Karen made no attempt to hide her interest. 'Why not both?'

'The current was too strong. Isn't it dreadful? Now he's gone abroad and left Hannah with her grandparents. I feel really sorry for her. She lives in London so she doesn't know anyone down here, she's got no-one to talk to.'

'So that's why we have to go to this garden party thing, only I don't see what use we'll be. Wouldn't she prefer someone her own age?'

They started walking. 'She's supposed to be clever,' said Laura. 'Perhaps she seems older than she actually is. Anyway, I told my grandmother I'd speak to her. We don't have to stay long.'

Laura had pointed out the Tremlett place before. It was down a road that gradually turned into a lane, with fields on both sides. The house and grounds were surrounded by a high wall so it was only possible to see the rooftops, but it was not difficult to imagine that there would be plenty of space for a couple of hundred people to wander round the garden, spending their money on silly games and stalls selling knitted rabbits and dried-up plants.

'It's not far,' said Laura. 'There's a short cut by that boarded-up church, then through the estate and on to North Road.'

'I'm in no hurry.' Karen had a stomach-ache, caused no doubt by Alex's home-made liver páte. 'You've met this Hannah, have you? On the way you can tell me what she's like, and fill me in on the rest of the family.'

'I only met her for the first time a couple of days ago, when Mrs Tremlett called round at my grandmother's to ask her to help with the teas. I don't really know anything about her.'

'Well, it's a pretty bad thing to happen, the drowning, I mean – only I don't suppose there's any mystery about it. I expect the red flag was flying but they ignored it. I know their type, more money than sense. Come on then, or we'll miss the Stick the Tail on the Donkey competition.'

The garden was seething with people. Children shouted and squealed as they played on the bouncy castle. A long queue waited impatiently outside the tea tent, trying to stay in the shade, although there wasn't much of it. Laura was trying to spot Hannah, or any other member of the Tremlett family who might know where she was.

'I can see her aunt,' she said. 'Fran Osborne. She runs some kind of sanctuary for wild animals. Look, over there.'

'Where? Can't see who you mean. What, lions and tigers? Lives near here, does she?'

'Out beyond the golf course. I've never been there and, as far as I can tell, it's only been going

9

a few months. She must have won the lottery or something. Oh, and that's Mr and Mrs Tremlett.' She pointed in the direction of the tea tent. 'Mrs Tremlett's the one with the long flowered dress. Mr Tremlett's very tall and—' She broke off suddenly and started hurrying across the grass. 'Look, there's Hannah. Over by the Lucky Dip.'

Karen shaded her eyes. 'The pale, skinny one with long fair hair?'

'Yes,' Laura said, then called to Hannah.

The girl looked frozen to the spot. Her eyes were darting round like a hunted animal's, then she saw Laura and managed an anxious smile.

'What are we supposed to say to her?' said Karen. It was a stupid question, but as far as she could remember it was the first time she had met someone whose mother had died only four months ago.

'Just treat her like anyone else,' said Laura crossly. 'Isn't that what you'd want if you were her?'

'Hallo, Laura.' Close to, Hannah looked even paler. 'Your grandmother said you might be coming. It's awfully crowded, isn't it? There was a queue even before they opened the gate. They're going to give the money to Christian Aid, only I thought they ought to give some of it to Fran, for the Rescue Centre.' She glanced at Karen, smiled briefly, then looked down at her blue flip-flops.

She was wearing jeans that were too short for her and a white T-shirt that had her name on the front and looked brand-new. Her hair had a dead-straight parting down the middle.

'How are you?' Laura's tone of voice made her sound like somebody's mother. 'This is Karen, a friend from school.' She gazed round the stalls. 'Have you won anything yet? Where's Silas?'

Hannah's face brightened a little. 'Shut up in the kitchen. He goes round sniffing people's legs so my grandmother said he'd have to stay in the house.'

'Silas is a black Labrador,' Laura explained.

'Oh, I see,' said Karen, 'I thought he was Hannah's grandfather.'

Laura glared at her. 'Let's go and see him. It'll be cooler inside.'

They entered the house through a door round

the back. While they were walking in single file, along the narrow stone-floored passage that led through to the kitchen, they met up with Hannah's aunt, Fran, carrying a box of tea bags. She recognised Laura; at least she was sure they had met before, but she couldn't recall her name.

'Your grandmother knows my mother, am I right? And you're . . .'

'Laura. And this is Karen. I was telling her about your animal sanctuary. It sounds really good.'

'The Rescue Centre? You must come and visit us.' Fran Osborne made an effort to appear cheerful and relaxed, but it didn't hide the fact that she looked tense and strained. Her round, rather flat face was covered in freckles, and everything about her – her coarse wavy hair, her eyes, even her cotton trousers and man's shirt – was brown. 'We haven't been going long so I'm afraid it's all in rather a muddle but . . . You've bikes, I expect, so it would only take you twenty minutes or so.'

'Thanks,' said Karen, 'we'd like that.'

'Good, any time then, and you can meet Dominic.'

As she moved off Karen noticed how the top half of her body was very long, compared with the shortness of her legs. She had put on a pair of sunglasses with thick dark frames. They made her look like an owl.

'Dominic's her son?' asked Karen.

Laura and Hannah exchanged glances, then both spoke at once. 'Stepson.'

'She's all right,' added Hannah, as though some explanation was required. 'I've another aunt, Sara, only she's quite different. You wouldn't think they were sisters.' She opened the kitchen door and the dog rushed out, pushing against each of them in turn, his tail thumping against the wall.

'Good boy.' Hannah pushed him back into the room, then took hold of his face in both hands and smoothed back his ears. 'Good boy, there's a good boy.'

Karen wanted to say how sorry she was about Hannah's mother. Talking about this and that, without ever mentioning what had happened, seemed crazy, but perhaps it would only make things worse. Instead, she asked a few questions about the dog. How old was he? Did he belong to Hannah or her grandparents? Did he need a lot of exercise?

Hannah answered politely, then suddenly looked up, let go of the dog, and started talking about her father. 'He's in Belgium, or I suppose he could be in Germany or Italy by now. He's away on business.'

'What kind of business?' asked Karen.

'Precision instruments.' Hannah spoke the words with pride. 'I'm not sure what he does exactly, but he's terribly clever, everyone says so.' Then afraid they might think she was boasting, 'Your father's an accountant, isn't he, Laura?'

'Yes, and Karen's is a private detective.'

'Oh!' Hannah put the tips of her fingers into her mouth. 'I mean, how interesting, like on television.'

'Not really,' said Karen. 'Anyway, why do people always say what their father does, never their mother?' As soon as she had spoken she realised her mistake. 'Oh, I'm sorry, Hannah, I didn't mean . . .'

'It's all right.' Hannah stood up and opened a cupboard, taking out three glasses and a large bottle of Coke. 'Actually the worst thing, when your mother dies, is that nobody speaks to you normally. They think they'd better be careful, so usually they say as little as possible.'

'Yes, I can see it might be like that,' said Karen. Surely it wasn't the worst thing about your mother dying, but she knew what Hannah meant. 'You're staying with your grandparents till next term, are you? Where d'you go to school?'

'In Putney, only I'm not sure when Dad'll be back.' She poured the Coke, filling the glasses too full so the bubbles came over the edge. 'Sorry, I always do that.' While she was fetching a cloth from the wooden draining-board she asked if they were going to visit Fran's Rescue Centre.

'Is it worth it?' said Laura. 'If it hasn't been going long, I don't suppose she's got many animals.'

'I don't know.' Hannah mopped up the Coke,

then dropped the cloth in the sink and wiped her hand on her jeans. 'I was going to go last week to see a badger, but it died. I think it had been hit by a car.'

Outside in the garden a loudspeaker was announcing the winners of a raffle. Laura stood up.

'Look, sorry about this, but I think I ought to go and speak to my grandmother. Her budgie's died and my mother says she's upset. No, you two stay here, I'll be back in ten minutes.'

After she left Karen and Hannah sat together in uncomfortable silence. In spite of the hot weather the kitchen felt cold, perhaps because of the stone floor and the smallness of the windows. There was a sour smell, perhaps of cheese, or it could have been milk that had been left out of the fridge and gone off.

Hannah yawned, putting up her hand to cover her mouth, then all of a sudden she leaned forward and started talking very fast. 'Your father, I hope you don't mind me asking, but has he always been a private detective?'

16

'No, he was in the police until a year or two back.'

'Oh, I see. Does he work by himself or has he got a partner?'

'On his own, although I sometimes help out if he's very busy.'

'Really?' Hannah rested her elbows on the table. 'You are lucky.'

'Well, I suppose so.' Karen was enjoying herself, even though she knew she was giving Hannah a totally false impression of what her father allowed her to do. 'Actually I was in the office most of last week, but now it's turned so hot he thinks I ought to get some fresh air. Anyway, there's not so much business this time of year.'

'What do you do actually?' Hannah's questions were beginning to sound more than just a way of making conversation.

'Oh, mainly tidying up, putting stuff into the computer.'

She nodded. 'I love computers. Daddy gave me his old one when I was six. You see, Mummy had to go out a lot so he thought . . .' She broke off, reaching for the dog, but he was lying flat out on the floor, asleep. 'What does your mother do?'

'Works in a gift shop. Expensive junk imported from all over the world. The shop used to be a church. It's quite near the cathedral, you may have seen it.'

Hannah tried to remember. 'Yes, I think I know where you mean. I thought she might work with your father.'

'They're divorced. My mother lives with this toy boy called Alex. Actually I was hoping to move in with my father but naturally no-one was that interested in what I wanted to do.'

'How awful.' Hannah's expression was deadly serious, then she smiled nervously. 'No-one talks about my mother any more, not in front of me. Sometimes I can hear them whispering. If I take off my shoes and creep towards the sitting-room I can usually catch a few words. They talk about *it*, never about my mother. Once Grandad used the name "Petra" but Granny said it was best for everyone, "especially Hannah", if *it* was forgotten.'

How could someone forget their mother? Still, Karen supposed what they meant was that it was no use going over and over the ways that Hannah's mother might have been saved – or Petra Tremlett saved and Hannah swept out to sea.

'If I stay in my bedroom,' said Hannah, 'they think I'm moping, so I play in the garden with Silas, then everyone's happy.'

Silas had started licking himself. Hannah bent down, inspecting the damp, straggly fur, and Karen felt a surge of pity. Hannah's mother had died and she was trying to protect other people from being too concerned about her.

'What d'you do all day?' asked Karen, 'apart from playing with Silas?'

'I don't know.' Hannah looked a little embarrassed. 'I fill in word puzzles, and those Test Your Own IQ books. I know it's stupid, but it helps to pass the time.'

'Have you got any pets of your own? In London, I mean.'

Hannah shook her head. 'Mummy said they make too much mess.' She felt in the pocket of her jeans and took out a picture postcard that had been folded in half. 'From my father, only there's something funny about it.' She chewed her lip. 'Oh, sorry. I mean you might want to go back to the garden party.'

'Let's have a look.' Karen smoothed out the picture of a fountain and some old stone buildings. She wanted to turn the card over, read what Hannah's father had written.

'Brussels,' said Hannah, 'posted four days ago, the day after the royal visit.'

'Royal visit?' The royal family was not one of Karen's special interests. It was one of the few things she and Alex agreed about.

'When the princess was taken ill,' said Hannah, 'and they had to get an ambulance. My father must have been there but he hasn't said anything about it and he knows I'm interested.'

Karen decided it would be all right to study the date stamp. She was slightly surprised to see that the card had been written in bright green ink. 'Perhaps he thought it wasn't worth mentioning,' she said.

'No, I'm sure that's not right.' Hannah's pale

face was flushed and her eyes were open very wide. 'I've got a scrapbook with pictures of her. The princess, I mean.' She rested her head on the table and when she spoke again her voice was slightly muffled. 'Anyway, it's not just that. Look, he says "weather could be better", but Grandad said it was hot all over Europe.'

'Well maybe your father doesn't like the heat.'

Hannah stared at her, keeping her eyes very wide open, as if she was afraid she might be going to cry. 'I don't think he's coming back, not ever. They won't tell me, they want to break it gently only nobody dares. "It's murder," that's what Grandad kept saying. Only I wasn't supposed to be listening.'

Karen swallowed hard. 'Murder? Oh, I don't expect he meant anything much. People often use that expression. I mean, they say it when something's very difficult – or unpleasant.'

Hannah moved her head from side to side. 'No, you don't understand. They all think Daddy killed her, only they'd never go to the police, so they've told him to stay away in case someone finds out, only I don't know—'

'But why? I mean, why would they think that?'

Hannah was sitting up, rubbing her eyes. 'Because of the argument.'

'What argument? Your parents had been fighting? Just before it happened? When you were on holiday in Devon?'

Hannah's whole body was shaking, but she kept her eyes fixed on Karen's face. 'I was in bed, but I could hear. Not just shouting, I think they were hitting each other. Then Mummy laughed. "Look at you," she said, "if you could see yourself, you're such a bloody . . ." Only I didn't hear the next bit.' She locked her fingers together, in an attempt to control the shaking. 'I wouldn't mind if someone would tell me the truth, only they won't, not ever, Granny wouldn't let them. The family, it's the most important thing in the world. You have to stick together whatever happens, it's the only thing that really matters.'

Two

'Sorry?' Alex leaned back in his deck chair, inviting Karen to repeat what she had just said. When she turned away he stretched out an arm. 'No, tell us all about it. It's just, your mother and I, we've a lot on our minds.'

'I won't disturb you then.' Karen enjoyed acting hard done by. It was stupid really since they always responded by giving her their undivided attention, which was certainly the last thing she wanted.

'Come on, love.' The skin on her mother's arm was peeling, on the soft fat part that was usually hidden under the sleeve of her T-shirt. 'You and Laura went to a summer fête and met this poor girl who'd lost her mother.'

'She was drowned at the end of April.'

'How terrible.'

'Yes, but it's not just that.' Karen had been wondering how much Hannah had witnessed. Had her grandfather really said 'it's murder', or had Hannah made this up to gain Karen's attention, or because she suspected her mother had been killed but had no actual evidence? Why, since they had only just met, had Hannah told her so much? For that very reason perhaps, because she was nothing to do with the Tremlett family, because it was easier to talk to a stranger. It occurred to Karen that Hannah's father might have gone away because he was afraid Hannah might know more than anyone else realised . . .

'Listen, love,' said her mother, 'we didn't have a chance to tell you before but Alex is applying for a new job.'

Karen sat down. 'Don't blame him. Get shot of that stupid Arts Centre. What kind of job?'

Her mother and Alex looked at each other, then Alex hauled himself into an upright position and ran his fingers through the new haircut that had replaced his scraggy ponytail. 'The thing is,

Karen, it would mean moving to Oxford.'

'But you could start at your new school only a few weeks into the autumn term,' said her mother, whose expression just recently had seemed stuck in a stupid grin. 'And you could come back and see Dad whenever you liked. So there's no need to worry about that.'

'I wasn't.' Karen was on her feet again and halfway into the house. 'The company on the first floor of his building has gone bust and their offices will soon be up for let. Dad's thinking of expanding so I'll be able to move in with him. One of those lucky coincidences, don't you think?'

The track that led up to the Rescue Centre was so bumpy that they had to get off their bikes and push them.

'Apparently it's got some silly name,' said Laura, 'and there's a board outside with a picture of a fox or something. You wouldn't think so to look at him, but Fran's husband, Trevor, is supposed to be artistic.'

'What do we call her? Mrs Osborne?'

Laura shrugged. 'Hannah just calls her Fran.'

A group of low, ramshackle buildings had come into view, and beyond them a rather ugly white house that looked in need of a coat of paint. There were fields all around but they were neglected, as if they had been farmed up to a year or so ago, then left to go wild.

'There you are,' said Laura, going up to the board and pointing at the picture. 'Tails and Whiskers, whoever thought that one up?'

Karen unlatched the gate. 'I expect it was to catch people's attention, like the television commercials that get on your nerves but you still can't help remembering the name of the product.'

'Yes, well it certainly looks as if they need to raise some money, and it must cost a fortune in vets' bills.'

There was no-one about but sounds were coming from one of the single-storey buildings. They left their bikes leaning against some iron railings, then Laura tapped on the door, but so softly that whoever was inside hadn't a hope of hearing.

'Push it open,' said Karen. 'I doubt if the animals are running loose. If they were there'd be a warning on the door.'

'What d'you want?' The voice had come from near the house, and a moment later a boy walked quickly towards them. He was tall, with black hair pushed behind his ears, and the kind of long dark lashes that people always say are wasted on a boy. Karen guessed he was about sixteen, or perhaps a little older, but whichever school he went to it wasn't the same one that she and Laura attended. He certainly wasn't the type that nobody notices, someone who gets lost in the crowd.

'Must be Dominic,' whispered Laura, then she called out, 'Mrs Osborne – Fran – she said we could come and visit whenever we liked.'

He caught up with them, then walked straight past, turning very briefly to look over his shoulder. 'Oh, you must be the kids she met at that stupid garden party thing. Does she know you're here?'

Fran came out of the low building, rubbing her hands on an old towel. 'Laura, how lovely to see you.'

27

'I wondered if we should have phoned, only you said—'

'No need for that.' In contrast to her stepson Fran seemed pleased, out of all proportion, that they had decided to take up her offer.

'You've met Dominic. Dominic, come and be introduced.' She waited for him, but a moment later he wrenched open the door to a small shed and disappeared. Fran shrugged. 'Must've got out of bed on the wrong side. Come and see my new rabbits.'

'Rabbits?' said Karen. 'You mean wild ones?'

Fran laughed. 'No, two big, white, fluffy Angoras. I'm trying to think up names so if you've any ideas ... We're planning on opening the place to the public. Oh, not this year, well, you can see how much work there is to do, but I'm starting to stock up on the kind of things children like. If the bunnies decide to start a family we're laughing.'

'You could have pony rides,' said Laura.

'Yes, good idea, if we can find the space for the ponies. A donkey, I'd certainly like to keep a donkey, but as Trevor keeps pointing out I mustn't lose sight of the real purpose of the place, to rescue wild creatures and nurse them back to health.'

They followed Fran into one of the sheds. Just before Karen closed the door behind them she noticed Dominic reappear, then cross the yard, carrying what looked like a dead crow in his hand although, on second thoughts, it could have been a black polythene bag.

The rabbits should have been out in the open, in a run. Karen disliked the way they sat crouched in their hutches, in the semi-darkness. The roof had several slates missing, but that seemed to be the only source of light. All the windows were boarded up, apart from one that was grey with cobwebs. A pile of broken wooden crates lay in one corner, together with the remains of a rusty piece of equipment, presumably left there since the time the place was a farm.

'No, don't tell me,' said Fran, opening a wire-covered door, lifting out a gigantic rabbit and handing it to Laura, 'this shed's quite unsuitable but they're only here till tomorrow. Trevor's almost completed their proper quarters. When you come again you'll be very impressed.'

Laura held the Angora against her body. Her face had assumed a dreamy look, then she noticed Karen's amused expression and passed the rabbit to her. Its back legs scrabbled hard, scratching the skin off Karen's arm, but she gritted her teeth and held on tight for several minutes before replacing it in the makeshift hutch and closing the door.

The next building contained the hospital room. An animal that could have been a stoat lay asleep in a pile of straw. It was curled up small but it was still possible to see that part of one of its back legs was missing.

'Wrenched off when it struggled to free itself from a trap,' said Fran. 'Peace and quiet, that's what they need when they first arrive. Plenty of warmth, plenty of liquids. Oh, don't worry this chap's been here over a week. Looks bad but he's doing pretty well, considering.'

There was something about the place that disturbed Karen. Perhaps it was the whole idea of rescuing animals from the wild. People liked to pretend dear little bunnies frolicked in the fields, when the truth was that everything lived off everything else. Birds ate insects, other birds ate those birds, or got eaten by foxes, then the foxes got hunted or shot by humans. Nature, red in tooth and claw; it was horrible but that was the way it was supposed to be.

Laura was gazing at a young hare. 'I think it's wonderful what you're doing,' she said. 'People find the animals and bring them to you, do they?'

'Yes, that's the general idea,' said Fran. 'It's taken time, of course, for people to hear about us, but the problem is, if we publicise ourselves too much we won't have the funds to cope. Later, when we're on our feet, we're hoping to open for school parties. Trevor says that way we might be able to get some kind of educational grant.'

'Good idea,' said Laura.

'Oh, yes, definitely,' Karen agreed. She was thinking about a boring school outing where the teachers had handed out questionnaires and a dopey girl called Tracy had filled in the word 'vulture' on the bird-spotting page.

'What about birds?' she asked Fran. 'I thought it wasn't much good trying to save them. My mother found a baby starling and put it in a box, but it died.'

'Yes, birds have a tendency to die of shock, poor things, but some of the larger ones . . .' And she was off on a story about a swan that had flown into overhead wires.

From Karen's point of view the purpose of the visit was to find out more about Hannah's parents, but how was she going to persuade Fran to talk about it? She could hardly ask straight out. *Hannah seems to think her father had something to do with her mother's death. Is that what you believe?*

They had left the hospital room and were walking towards a small shed that smelled like overflowing dustbins on a hot summer's day. Not that the weather was all that warm. It had changed in the night and rain was forecast by the evening. Karen looked round, hoping to see Fran's husband Trevor, someone outside the Tremlett family who might be more prepared to talk about the tragedy.

'Trevor's building new quarters for the animals,' said Fran. 'Don't know what I'd do without him, there's nothing he can't turn his hand to. Of course, if I have to go away he can take over the livestock, no trouble at all.'

'You've only been open a few months, haven't you?'

Fran nodded. 'Since January.'

So if Fran had accompanied the family on their Devon holiday Trevor must have stayed behind. That meant he would know nothing about the events that had taken place leading up to Hannah's mother being drowned. And nothing about what happened in the sea. Had Dominic gone with them? Somehow Karen thought that was unlikely.

He was crossing the yard again, this time without the dead animal.

'Ah, there you are,' said Fran, as if he had been missing for hours. 'Now don't rush off, I want you to meet Laura and Karen. Margaret Wolfenden is Laura's grandmother.'

'Oh, yes.' Dominic couldn't have sounded less interested. 'I'll be going into town soon, want me to buy some bread? There was none left this morning, I had to eat those disgusting oatcake things.'

'Oh, thanks, Dommie.' Fran beamed at him. 'And a few other things if you can manage it.' She took a scrap of paper out of the pocket of her old tweed jacket and start scribbling with a ballpoint that seemed to be running out of ink.

Dominic was looking Karen and Laura up and down, as if he were inspecting a couple of horses that might, or might not, be up to the standard he required. 'Right, I'm off,' he said, snatching the paper from his stepmother's hand. 'Dad's having trouble with the electric drill. I should stay well clear.'

An old Volvo estate car was parked at the far end of the yard, and a short distance away a motor-bike that looked about the same age. As they watched, Dominic climbed on to the bike, revved up the engine, then shot across the yard and out through the gate, only slowing down when he reached the worst of the potholes in the lane.

'Sixteenth birthday a couple of weeks ago,' explained Fran. 'Trevor thought he deserved a bit of a treat.'

Karen didn't think he deserved anything.

Rude, arrogant, patronising, the list was endless.

'Oh, Dom's all right,' said Fran, aware that Karen and Laura must have received a rather unfavourable impression of her stepson. 'Taking a bit of time to settle in. As I say, we've only been here since just after Christmas.'

'Hannah's fond of animals,' said Karen. She had no evidence for this, apart from the way she seemed to have attached herself to the black Labrador. 'I mean, she's very fond of Silas, although she said she wasn't allowed any pets at home.'

Fran's expression had changed dramatically. She was clenching and unclenching her jaw, and the water in the bowl in her hand was dripping on to the ground.

'You've talked to Hannah then. When was that? Oh, of course, the day of the garden party. What did she say?'

'Nothing in particular.' Karen was watching Fran carefully.

'No, silly question, it's just – well, we worry about her, the whole family does, but I suppose that's only natural. She was going to visit us up here but it had to be put off. I'm hoping she'll arrange to come again, but it's not very easy at present.'

What wasn't very easy?

'She could come with us if you like,' said Karen, ignoring the way Laura was staring at her. 'If that would be all right with you, I mean.'

'Yes, of course.' Fran was beaming again. 'How kind of you. If it wouldn't be too much of a bore I'm sure my mother would be delighted. Now, let me show you my beautiful owl. Broke a wing but the vet says she'll soon be good as new.'

On the way home they barely spoke to one another. It was partly because the lane was so rough it was impossible to cycle side by side, but it wasn't just that. Karen wondered if the tension between them was because Laura was annoyed with her for mentioning Hannah, and how her mother hadn't allowed her to keep any pets.

'It's no good pretending she never existed,' she said, jumping off her bike as they approached the main road, then leaning it against a wall.

'Pretending who never existed?' Laura was

watching the gathering clouds. 'Oh, you're not still on about Petra Tremlett. Hannah needs people who'll cheer her up, not keep going on and on about what happened.'

'I didn't go on and on. She was the one who brought up the subject. Anyway, how d'you know that's what she wants? She might prefer it if she was allowed to talk without people changing the subject all the time.'

'Is that what she said?'

'Not exactly.' For some reason she had decided not to tell Laura how Hannah had overheard her parents fighting – the day before her mother drowned. 'Did Fran go to Devon? Surely if it was only April it can't have been warm enough for them to go swimming in the sea.'

'Yes, it was, you remember that heat wave which started at the end of the month and continued halfway through May?'

'I forget.' Karen tried to sound as casual as possible, but it was unlikely she would deceive Laura. 'Anyway, the reason I asked, I just wondered how many of the family were staying there at the time.'

'Why d'you want to know?'

'Oh, no reason in particular, only if we're going to take Hannah with us to the Rescue Centre the more we know about it the better. I mean, that way I won't put my foot in it, say something that upsets her.'

Laura was looking at her suspiciously. 'According to my grandmother, they all went except Trevor and Dominic. Fran only married Trevor last year and there was some fuss about it.'

'What kind of fuss?'

Laura shrugged. 'I haven't a clue.'

'So it would have been Mr and Mrs Tremlett, Fran, Hannah and her parents, and the other aunt, what's she called?'

'Sara. Why?'

Karen shrugged. 'Just wondered.'

'She lives in London.'

'Is she married?'

'I've no idea. No, I don't think so. Look, if we see Hannah again, please don't keep talking about what happened, just stick to the animals, it's obvious that's what everyone wants.'

'Everyone?' said Karen, then she noticed Laura's expression and decided it was better to change the subject. 'Anyway, what d'you think of that Dominic?'

Laura pulled a face. 'Awful, isn't he? I feel sorry for Fran, it's not as though he's even her real son.'

'He's certainly got a high opinion of himself.'

'Well, I suppose he is quite good-looking.'

'Oh, you thought so, did you?'

They laughed to cover up the awkward moment, then climbed on their bikes, turned down the short cut, ignoring the 'No Cycling' notice, and set off towards the city centre.

Three

Karen's father was too busy to answer her questions. These days he was nearly always too busy. And she hadn't even got round to telling him her plan about taking over the first floor of the building and turning it into a flat where the two of them could live.

The phone rang again and he picked it up impatiently. 'Cady's Detective Agency. Bob Cady speaking.' But as soon as the caller answered Karen could tell it was personal. He put his hand over the mouthpiece and mouthed the word 'coffee', which was his way of saying he wanted her out of the room.

Half closing the door behind her, she walked noisily towards the tiny kitchen, then crept back and stood outside the office, listening. 'Friday evening? Yes, I don't see why not . . . That new restaurant down by the river? Yes, I think I know where you mean . . . Oh, just before you go, Judy – no, it doesn't matter, tell you when I see you . . . Yes, me too. Bye, then. Bye.'

Judy? For a dreadful moment Karen thought he might have been talking to her mother's friend, Jude, who worked with her in the gift shop. Surely not. Jude was the size of a bus, with horse's teeth, and a voice that droned on and on and . . .

'Oh, there you are, what a surprise.' Her father had opened the door and was staring at her, without smiling. Then his long, thin face broke into a grin. 'All right, nosey, so I took your advice and made an effort to improve my social life.'

'Good, I'm really glad. Look, I wasn't listening, not really, it was just that I couldn't help hearing the name Judy and I thought . . .'

'Go on.'

'Well, you know Mum's friend at the shop . . .?'

'Jude? I take it you *are* joking?'

'Forget it. Listen, did Mum tell you, Alex is applying for a job in Oxford? Anyway, I've told them I haven't the slightest intention of going with them so—'

'Hang on, not so fast, your mother's thinking of moving away?'

Karen nodded. 'Anyway, the thing is—'

'First I've heard of it. Look, I have to go out now but we'll talk about it later.'

'Yes, all right.' *Talk about it later.* That sounded quite hopeful. 'Oh, Dad, just before you go. If you held someone's head under the water till they drowned would anyone be able to prove it was murder?'

He rubbed his moustache. 'Not unless there were bruises on the body, something suggesting a struggle. Even then it would be difficult to demonstrate the marks hadn't been caused by knocking against the side of the pool or—'

'Oh, not in a swimming-pool, I was talking about the sea.'

Her father paused in the doorway. 'You were talking about the sea,' he repeated. 'What is this, some book you've been reading?'

She nodded. 'I just thought it didn't sound very convincing. Anyway, it doesn't matter. I'll call in next week, shall I, so we can have a really good talk. Oh and by the way, enjoy yourself on Friday evening.'

It was Laura's birthday and everyone had given her money. She and Karen trailed round the shopping centre inspecting racks of clothes, but without much enthusiasm. The hot weather had returned and it was impossible to imagine feeling cold enough to need a jumper, let alone the grey zip-up jacket that Laura had been intending to buy.

'Why not spend it all on lottery tickets,' said Karen, 'then, when you win the jackpot, we can join Tessie in Orlando.'

'They won't sell them to people our age.'

'Want to bet?'

'Is that what you'd like to do? Visit Disney World?'

'I might.' Laura was so boringly sensible. Karen missed Tessie – or did she? They had been close friends since primary school, even though they were so different. Tessie was an extrovert, always squealing with excitement or bursting into tears, looking in the mirror, fussing about her hair. Maybe being with Laura made a pleasant change. Maybe Karen was never satisfied.

'Look.' Laura was pointing across the road.

'What? Oh, that stupid bloke with green hair standing up in waxy points.'

'No, not him. Over by the bookshop.'

It was Mrs Tremlett and Hannah. Karen would never have recognised Ginny Tremlett, but she remembered the flowered dress and white shoes. She had a large number of shopping bags and she was leaning against a wall, talking and laughing. Hannah looked miserable.

'Go and speak to them, shall we?' said Karen, and before Laura could answer she had hurried across the road.

'Karen!' Hannah sounded gratifyingly pleased to see her. Then she turned to her grandmother. 'This is Karen and Laura, they came to the garden party.'

'Well, of course I know Laura, darling. Nice to meet you, Karen. Hannah's told me all about you.'

'Really? There's not much to tell.'

Mrs Tremlett smiled. 'About your father, I mean. What an interesting job, although I dare say he sees a side of life the rest of us would prefer not to know about.'

Hannah was wearing a blue denim pinafore dress and a blue-and-white check shirt. It made her look different, less waif-like, more sure of herself, but Karen was certain the difference was only skin deep.

'We went to see Tails and Whiskers,' said Laura, 'there's a beautiful barn owl. Fran – I mean, Mrs Osborne – says they'll be able to set it free quite soon.'

'Yes, it's noble work she's doing,' said Mrs Tremlett. A minute ago she had seemed in no particular hurry, now she couldn't wait to start moving away.

'We could take Hannah with us if you like,' suggested Karen. 'If she'd like to come, that is. Actually we were hoping to go tomorrow afternoon, to see if the stoat's better. Shall we pick Hannah up on the way? Has she got a bike? Or we wouldn't mind walking, would we Laura? It's not all that far.'

'That's kind,' said Mrs Tremlett, 'but I'm afraid Hannah's going with me to meet a friend tomorrow afternoon. What a shame. Still, another day I'm sure we could fix something up.'

Karen glanced at Hannah, then back at Mrs Tremlett. Hannah's grandmother was probably about sixty-five. Her hair was wavy and almost white, cut to just below her ears, and she had very bright blue eyes. In spite of her cheerful expression Karen wasn't sure she liked the look of her. Not because she was trying to prevent Hannah from visiting the Rescue Centre with them, but because she smiled too much. When Alex first came to live with them her mother had done just the same. Now that he had applied for the job in Oxford, she was doing it again. Smiling designed to put you in a double bind: *See, you can't kick up all that fuss, not when I'm being so friendly, so reasonable.*

Ginny Tremlett seemed set on giving the impression that she was a pleasant, easy-going kind of person, but what would she be like if she didn't get her own way? She was rearranging her shopping bags, stretching out her fingers where the handles had made ridges on her skin.

'I tell you what,' she said, suddenly changing her mind for no apparent reason, apart from the fact that Karen and Hannah were both staring her out, 'I'll visit Evelyn on my own, Hannah, and you go to the Rescue Centre with Laura and her friend.'

'Great. Two o'clock all right?' asked Karen.

'Two o'clock would be fine.' Mrs Tremlett started to walk away, then stopped abruptly, calling to Karen and Laura over her shoulder. 'Hang on a moment, you two, I'm sure Hannah would like you to meet her other aunt.'

A tall woman in her late thirties, with very short dark hair, had come out of a nearby shop.

'My daughter, Sara,' said Ginny Tremlett. 'Sara, this is Laura, Margaret's granddaughter, and . . .' She turned to Karen. 'I'm so sorry, I've forgotten your name.'

'Karen Cady,' said Hannah, surprising Karen, who had no idea that Hannah knew her surname.

Sara shook hands with each of them. Karen remembered Hannah mentioning that her two aunts looked very different. That was an understatement. Where Fran was short and dumpy, Sara was tall and elegant. Her hair was cut in the kind of style that has to be trimmed every couple of weeks. Everything about her was smart, expensive, not just her clothes, but the brown leather handbag with its zips and pockets, the silver rings, the bracelets, even the watch displayed on her long, thin wrist.

Karen had become uncomfortably aware that her mouth might be hanging open, just a little. She hated the idea that Sara Tremlett might think she was impressed by her expensive get-up.

'Yes, well, we'd better go.' She turned towards Sara. 'Nice to meet you, and we'll see you tomorrow, Hannah.'

Hannah was standing on one leg, pressing her lips together as if she was trying to control a fit of nervous giggling.

'Two o'clock,' she managed to mutter. 'Thanks.'

Karen had no idea how long Sara Tremlett was staying with her parents. Certainly she never expected to see her again that same day. It was early evening and she was exercising a dog belonging to a neighbour who was away on holiday. Since the creature was twelve years old, and grossly overweight, exercising was the wrong word. She held on to the lead and the dog sniffed at every blade of grass surrounding each tree in the street.

She had been hoping to take it by the river, but it was too slow, it would have taken an age to drag it there and back. Instead, she was standing at the top of the steps that led down to the quayside, trying to get the dog moving again without pulling its collar over its head.

Across the other side of the water a girl was standing on the balcony of one of the flats, waving to a friend. Her long fair hair reminded Karen of Hannah, not that she needed any reminding. Ever since the conversation in the kitchen at the Tremletts' house she had longed for another opportunity to talk to her. Everyone, including Laura, seemed to think it was best not to mention the tragedy, but was that because they wanted to protect Hannah, or because talking about it made *them* feel bad?

Of course, it was possible that Hannah's description of her parents' argument the night before the drowning was a lie, or at the very least an exaggeration. She was angry with her father for going away and wanted to blame him for her mother's death. But that couldn't be right. One of the things that was upsetting her so much was the fear that he had gone away and might never come back.

Something about the Tremlett family made Karen uneasy. Fran, who had become so agitated when Karen just happened to mention that she and Hannah had talked to each other for a short time. Mrs Tremlett, Hannah's grandmother, who had seemed so unwilling to allow Hannah to accompany them to the Rescue Centre. Laura would have said Karen was imagining it, trying to create a mystery where none existed, but maybe the whole family were ganging up, trying to hide the truth about what had happened on that day in Devon. What was it Hannah had said, quoting her grandmother's words? *The family, it's the most important thing in the world. You have to stick together, whatever happens.*

Karen had decided it was up to her to help Hannah as much as she could. Wasn't that exactly what Hannah had been asking her to do when she showed her the postcard, then recounted the conversation between her grandparents? *'It's murder.' That's what I heard Grandad saying.* Karen had done her best to reassure Hannah, but they both knew there was something wrong. Hannah was intelligent, perceptive, and she could recognise the difference between people who wanted to protect her from more unhappiness, and relatives who needed to protect themselves from a family scandal. A murder?

Bending down to get a grip on the thick hair at the back of the dog's neck, Karen spotted two figures standing near the place where the ferry crossed over. One she recognised instantly. The blue loose-fitting trousers and white jacket, the long, delicate hands with their rings flashing in the sun. The other was a man, who had parked his purple sports car on the double yellow lines. He had fair hair, receding at the temples, which looked as if it had been brushed back and kept in place with lashings of gel. He was of average height, but not as tall as Sara Tremlett, and he was dressed in a light grey suit with a shirt and tie, and carrying a black briefcase.

The two of them were talking animatedly, like close friends who haven't seen each other for quite a time – or were they having some kind of argument? Suddenly the man jumped into the car without bothering to open the driver's door, reversed dangerously fast for a few metres, then did a U-turn and came up the slope, fairly close to where Karen was still standing, and joined the traffic on the dual carriageway.

A driver hooted loudly and Karen saw the man in the purple sports car raise one finger. When she looked back at the quayside she expected Sara to have disappeared, but she was still there and she was staring up the steps. A moment later she bounded up them, two at a time.

Karen froze. Had Sara seen her? Did she think she had been spying on her? But why would she want to do that? The best thing was to start walking, then, if Sara caught up with her, she could feign surprise.

'It's Karen, isn't it?' The voice was harsh but when Karen turned round Sara's face was expressionless.

'Yes, that's right.' Karen tried to look puzzled. She could smell Sara's perfume, it was the one that Alex had given Karen's mother for her birthday, or did they all smell much the same? 'Oh, yes, we met at the shopping centre. I'm taking a neighbour's dog for a walk. They're on holiday, in Barbados, I think.' She broke off, realising she was talking too much.

'How kind of you.'

'Not really, I'm getting paid for it.'

Sara smiled. 'You live near here, do you? I'm afraid I'm hopeless at finding my way about. My parents moved down several years ago but of course I was living in London by then. Anyway,' she paused for breath, 'I wanted to discover the quickest way to that new bridge over the river, the one that bounces when you walk on it. My father was telling me about it. Apparently it's perfectly safe, but—'

'Yes, but it's not really that new. It was called the New Bridge when it was built about five years

54

ago and the name seems to have stuck.'

What did Sara Tremlett want? She was being quite friendly, but there was a coldness in her eyes and Karen doubted she would have run all the way up the steps just to make pleasant conversation.

As Karen watched Sara pulled one of the rings off her finger, then pushed it back on again. 'Anyway,' she said, trying to sound as casual as possible, but only giving the impression she was incredibly tense, 'I thought I'd have a quick word, just in case you were wondering . . . That man you saw me with. He stopped his car, probably saw me looking lost.'

'Yes, I expect so.' Why did Sara feel the need to explain? And the way she was going about it, how could anyone have believed what she was saying?

'Anyway, I'm sure we'll meet again,' she said. 'I'm so glad you and Laura have decided to befriend poor Hannah. She must be a bit younger than you are.'

It irritated Karen the way people kept describing her as 'poor Hannah'.

'I like her,' she said. 'Oh by the way, the purple car, you don't happen to know what make it was, do you, only my father's very keen on sports cars and I've never seen one quite like that before.'

Sara's eyes narrowed. 'I've absolutely no idea,' she said coldly, 'but I strongly advise you to forget you ever saw it. People don't like being spied on, you know, and I've given you a perfectly good explanation as to why I was down on the quay.'

Four

It had rained hard in the night. The lane leading up to the Rescue Centre had water in the potholes and the overhanging trees dripped on to their heads. It was easier to push their bikes than try and avoid all the bumps. Hannah was wearing a pink anorak and her hair was in one long thin plait. She looked very pale.

'I don't expect you wanted to come. I mean, with Laura having a temperature and everything.'

'Yes I did,' said Karen. 'Anyway, she'll probably be all right by tomorrow, just a cold, she's always getting coughs and colds.'

'I used to have a weak chest,' said Hannah, 'at least that's what my mother always said, but I think it was just an excuse so she didn't have to

57

take me out with her. This woman used to come round, like a sort of nanny, except she never actually stayed the night.'

'Didn't you like her?'

Hannah thought about it for a moment. 'She was all right. She used to make me wash my hands a lot, and only drink water after I'd finished eating.'

'Why?'

'I don't know really. Grandad says I don't eat enough. He's always talking about nutrition and fibre content.'

'That's because he's a doctor.' A buzzard was hovering over the field on the left. With a sudden swoop it pounced on whatever it had been watching, then rose into the sky with its victim in its claws.

Karen pointed at it, but Hannah seemed to have no interest. 'I never eat much at meals,' she said. 'I think it's because they're always watching me. But I buy chocolate at a shop near the roundabout, and eat it in my bedroom.'

'Oh, yes, well, if you don't like the meals . . .'

Hannah seemed to have this great wish to

confess her sins. Perhaps the illicit chocolate eating made her feel she lived in a lonely world of her own.

'No, it's not that. Granny buys a lot of those chilled pre-cooked meals, then adds things to them so Grandad thinks they're home-made.'

So Mrs Tremlett had her good points after all. 'Hannah, you know the day your mother drowned?'

Hannah looked at her gratefully. 'I'm so glad you don't mind talking about it. I keep going over and over it in my mind. It looked very sunny but I suppose the water was quite cold, except you get used to it after a bit, don't you? You see, the thing is, they didn't really want me to go swimming.'

'Who didn't?'

She hesitated. 'Daddy, I think. And Fran said skinny people like me had a habit of turning blue if they swam in the sea. She's a good swimmer.'

'Fran is?'

Hannah nodded vigorously. 'I know she's quite – well, she's not exactly slim, but I think that can be an advantage, and she's got very strong arms.'

'What about Sara?' asked Karen.

'Oh, she's good at everything. Anyway,' she turned her head sharply so Karen couldn't see the expression on her face, 'if I'd stayed on the beach . . .'

'Look, you don't know that, Hannah. Everyone talks as if your father had to choose which of you he saved, but it mightn't have been like that, I mean he mightn't have been able to save your mother anyway.'

'No, I suppose not.' Karen's words didn't seem to have consoled her very much. 'You know I told you how they all keep whispering and I thought it was because they didn't want to upset me?'

'Yes, you said.'

'Well, I don't think it's just that. I think they know something awful and they want to make sure I never find out what it is. D'you think I'm being silly?'

'No, but I think you may have got it wrong, what your grandfather said – about it being murder.'

'Oh, that.' She sighed heavily. 'But it's other things, too.'

'What things?'

But they had reached the gates to the centre and Hannah wasn't going to tell her any more. Later perhaps, but not until she knew there was no risk of being overheard.

'Did you see Dominic?' Hannah asked. 'I mean, last time you and Laura came here?'

'We saw him,' said Karen, in a voice that made Hannah smile. 'You've known him ever since your aunt married his father, have you?'

'Oh, no, long before that.' She seemed surprised by Karen's question. 'Trevor used to bring him sometimes – to play in the garden. The first time I saw him I think I was eight, so he must have been about the same age I am now.'

Rain was dripping off the Tails and Whiskers board, but the sky was starting to clear and Karen could feel her spirits rising. She was sorry Laura felt ill but at least it meant she was having an opportunity to speak to Hannah on her own, although she would have to be careful what she said. Just allowing Hannah to talk about everything under the sun would be the best way of finding out as much as possible.

Fran was coming out of the house, dragging a heavy bag. She waved to them, called something neither of them could catch, then hauled the bag into one of the sheds.

'I wonder what's inside,' said Hannah. 'You don't think . . . I hate it when animals die.'

'Looked more like feedstuff,' said Karen hopefully, an unwelcome memory returning. The first pet she had ever had, her long-haired Peruvian guinea-pig, lying on its side, wheezing. In the morning it had been dead.

Hannah was staring at her. 'Sometimes I'm quite glad I haven't got any pets,' she said. 'Anyway, there's no-one in our house in London, so if we'd had a cat or something I don't know what would have happened to it.'

Karen took Hannah's bike and leaned it against a wall, then the two of them went to join Fran in the shed. As soon as they opened the door the smell hit them in the face, a strong, musky scent that reminded Karen of the porcupine enclosure at the zoo.

'Hi.' Fran pushed back her hair with the back of her gloved hand. 'Glad you could make it.

Come and have a look at our latest addition.'

The fox was lying on a heap of straw. Its eyes were closed, but now and again they opened for a second, then drooped shut again.

Hannah drew in a breath. 'What's the matter with it?'

'Not sure,' said Fran. 'Vet's coming out in an hour or so. Brought in by a woman who found it in her garden, lying under a hedge. Think she's expecting cubs.'

'Laura's got a temperature,' said Karen, 'so it's just the two of us.'

'Oh, I'm sorry about that. I've one or two jobs for you, if that's all right. Just general clearing up, but I need all the help I can get.'

'Yes, of course.' Karen wondered if the previous owner of the place had gone bankrupt and Fran and her husband had bought it fairly cheaply. Why had Laura thought there was some kind of fuss when Fran got married? It was one of the things she would have to prise out of Hannah, but not yet. First Karen needed to convince Fran how useful it was having her and Hannah round the place.

'What would you like us to do?' she asked.

'Oh, goodness me, there's so much, I hardly know where to tell you to start.' Fran thought about it for a moment, then suggested they collect up some of the rubbish that was lying about in a disused barn. 'I want to make it into a stable,' she said, 'somewhere for the goats to go if it turns nasty next winter.'

'Fine.' Karen had her hand on the door. 'Coming, Hannah?'

But Hannah wanted to stay with the fox. The sight of it had brought tears to her eyes, but maybe that wasn't such a bad thing. Apart from the occasional burst of nervous laughter, she seemed numbed by the accident. Would Karen have reacted the same way if *her* mother had died? She thought about Tessie (even now having her picture taken with a larger-than-life Mickey Mouse – or was it the middle of the night in Florida?). Tessie would have cried buckets for weeks, then started to feel a whole lot better. Karen would have gone quiet, like Hannah. They were similar in lots of ways, two of a kind, or was she just imagining it?

While Karen was clearing the barn a small, bearded man put his head round the door, then negotiated a path between the piles of mouldy straw and broken bricks. He was dressed in a tartan shirt, with one sleeve coming away at the shoulder, and what was left of his hair was very dark.

'Trevor,' he said, holding out a hand. 'And you're . . .?'

'Karen Cady. I came with Hannah. She's looking at the fox.'

'Ah, the fox. What d'you think of the place, then? Going to take a while to make it a going concern. Fran's got all these big ideas about visitors who'll contribute to the upkeep, but you can't expect them to come when there's only a handful of animals.'

Karen wanted to sound as interested as possible. In a way it was true, she was interested. Her misgivings about saving injured animals were starting to change. She had never thought of herself as sentimental, but if she tried too hard she could easily end up at the other extreme, like that friend of her father's who wanted all

Beatrix Potter books banned because the animals were dressed in clothes.

'What happens if the animals get too tame to be returned to the wild?' she asked.

Trevor left the barn and she followed him into the yard. 'Good question,' he said. 'Something we'll have to avoid as far as possible. Of course for young animals, with no memory of their territory, you have to have special release schemes.' He was knotting a broken lace in one of his boots. 'You're a friend of Hannah's, are you?'

'Not exactly a friend,' she said, 'we only met last week.'

'Poor kid.' He sat on an upturned dustbin. 'I'd like to help, but I doubt if anything I said would be much good.' He sounded genuinely sympathetic, not patronising like the rest of them. 'Dreadful thing to happen. Fran was there at the time, holidaying with the family in North Devon.'

'But you stayed here, to look after the animals.'

He nodded. 'Not exactly number one favourite with the Tremlett family. Never come near us up here, but I can't say it bothers me.'

'Mr and Mrs Tremlett, they never come and see the centre?'

'Leo saw it once, when the business side was being tied up. You want to watch yourself, coming out without a hat with colouring like that,' he said suddenly, then continued: 'Met Mrs Tremlett senior, have you? Doesn't approve of me at all. Still, can't really blame her. As for Dominic . . . Anyway, where is he? Gone off again, I suppose, afraid he might be asked to do some work.'

'His bike's still here.'

'So it is. And you won't catch Dominic walking into town.' He yawned loudly. 'Time for a cup of tea. Want one?'

'Oh, right. Thanks.'

'You never knew Hannah's mother then?' He scratched the bald patch on the back of his head. 'Hannah takes after her father. Oh, I'm not saying she won't turn out quite pretty in a year or two. I was thinking more about her personality. A wild one, that Petra was, and could be nasty with it. Treated me as beneath contempt.'

He paused, waiting for Karen to ask why.

When she said nothing he continued anyway.

'Well, she'd bettered herself, hadn't she, turned herself into one of the nobs. Prided herself on her taste in furniture and interior decor, as she liked to call it.' He picked up a heavy wooden mallet and swung it in one hand. 'Needed to be the centre of attention, did Petra, and if she found she wasn't—' He broke off, looking towards the house. 'Well, I should know. Dominic's mother wasn't all that different. Wouldn't surprise me if she ended up the same way.'

Dominic and Hannah were coming out of the fox's quarters. Hannah hurried across to join her.

'It's looking a bit better, Karen. It tried to stand up, only its legs are all wobbly. D'you think it's going to be all right?'

'I wouldn't count on it.' Dominic was staring at Karen with the same irritatingly superior expression as before. His voice was equally condescending. 'Can't stay away from the place, eh? What's the big attraction? Hannah tells me your friend's ill in bed. Pity, I was rather hoping we'd meet up again.'

He disappeared into the house, leaving Hannah so red in the face it made Karen laugh.

'Everything he says makes me furious.'

'Oh, take no notice,' said Karen, 'just a pathetic show off. I've met his type before.'

'Yes, I know.' Hannah wiped her hands on her red T-shirt. 'When we were looking at the fox he kept saying things.'

'What kind of things?'

She hesitated. 'Mostly about Dad.'

'Your father?' This was interesting, but she would have to be careful. 'D'you mean he deliberately tried to upset you?'

'Just now he asked if my parents had argued a lot, had big rows.'

'What did you say?'

'Nothing. And he wanted to know if Dad was stronger than he looks – and if he's a good swimmer.'

Karen wanted to go straight into the house and tell Dominic what she thought of him. Instead, she advised Hannah to take no notice, just make sure she stayed well clear of him. 'He's a born trouble-maker, you only have to look at him. If you're on your own and he comes up to you again, just walk away. By the way, what happened to his mother?'

Hannah's face was deadly serious. 'It was awful. She ran off with a man she met in a bar. They were in Italy, on holiday. Trevor had to come back on his own.' She felt in her pocket. 'I know we're supposed to be having a cup of tea, only I wondered if you'd like to see these.' She held out several photographs. 'I wanted to show you because you're the only one who doesn't treat me as if I'm funny in the head.'

'Oh, come on, Fran's all right. Let's have a look, then.'

The photos looked like old ones but it turned out they had been taken when the family was on holiday in April. 'I keep them in my pocket,' Hannah explained, 'that's why some of them have got a bit bent. It's silly really, but I don't want someone finding them and throwing them away.'

'Why on earth would anyone do that?' Pointing to an elegant figure in a white swimming costume, Karen said, 'That's Sara, isn't it? And the man standing next to her . . .?'

'That's Daddy. His name's Jonathan. He's quite tall, but he looks even taller because he's so skinny, like me.' She held out another photo. 'And that's my mother, only it's not very good of her. She had blonde hair, much nicer than mine, and she didn't even colour it.'

'She was very attractive.' Karen hated using the past tense, but she didn't want to fall into the same trap as the rest of the family, talking as if the drowning had never happened.

Hannah nodded. 'Yes, that's what everyone said. Those people in the background, they're Fran and my grandparents. Have you met my grandfather? His real name's Leonard but everyone calls him Leo. He used to be a heart specialist but he's retired now, only I don't think he likes it. I mean, he gets a bit bad-tempered, and he's funny with Silas.'

'How d'you mean?'

'If Granny's there he pats Silas and pretends to really like him, but when she goes out of the room he gives him a kick and calls him a filthy mutt.'

Karen laughed, encouraging Hannah to keep talking. She wanted time to study the photographs, especially the picture of the whole family, apart from Leo Tremlett, who must have been holding the camera. Behind the group, and slightly concealed by a beach hut, was a man wearing a dark jacket and trousers, and a white shirt buttoned up at the neck. Because it was obviously a hot day he stood out from the rest of the holidaymakers in their brightly-coloured shorts and swimming costumes.

'Who's that?' she asked, indicating the man.

Hannah peered at the figure. 'I don't know. Just someone on the beach, I suppose. Why?'

Just someone on the beach. But Karen was almost certain she had seen him before. The same slicked down hair, trendy suit. He was the man with the purple sports car, the man who had been talking to Sara Tremlett.

Alex answered the phone. 'For you, Karen,' he called, 'someone called Mrs Tremlett. Have I got the name right?'

'Yes.' Karen's hands were trembling. Had

Hannah said something about the photo on the beach?

'Ginny Tremlett speaking, Karen. I do hope you didn't mind me ringing, Laura's mother gave me your number, only I wanted to thank you – for being so kind to Hannah. She's had such a terrible few months, and now, with her father away and everything . . .'

'That's all right, I don't mind at all. We're going to help Fran tidy up the Rescue Centre.'

'Yes.' There was a long pause. 'That's really the reason I'm ringing. Hannah's always been so sensitive, not that there's anything wrong with that.' She paused again.

What was she trying to say? That Hannah had a tendency to invent things? That anything she told Karen . . .

Mrs Tremlett cleared her throat noisily. 'Well, I suppose what I wanted to say is, I wouldn't like you to feel you *have* to let Hannah tag along because of what's happened to her.'

'I don't, Mrs Tremlett. We seem to get on pretty well. I expect it's because we both like animals.'

'Yes, well, that's very nice, of course.'

Was she trying to warn Karen off seeing Hannah again? If so, the conversation was having exactly the opposite effect.

Mrs Tremlett's falsely friendly voice came back on the line. 'Well, as long as you remember children in her situation do tend to let their imaginations run away with them. I suppose it's because the truth is sometimes too hard to bear. We're worried about her – she's not eating properly. I thought perhaps you might be able to get through to her. Oh, and just one last thing, if she says anything you feel we ought to know about I'm sure you wouldn't hesitate to get in touch.'

'Of course.' Like hell, she would.

What did they think Hannah was going to tell her? Karen felt certain she wouldn't have told her grandparents how she had heard her parents having an argument. It *must* be the photo. She must have asked her grandmother about the man by the beach hut, and for some reason Mrs Tremlett wanted to make sure Karen never found out who he was. Or did Ginny Tremlett

74

know her son, Jonathan, had murdered his wife, and she was desperately worried that Hannah might have seen enough to realise the drowning hadn't been an accident?

'Don't worry, Mrs Tremlett,' she said brightly, 'I'm sure what you're saying is right. I'll try and get her to concentrate on the animals. There's a fox that's going to have cubs and a bat with a damaged wing. You should go up there yourself sometime. It's very interesting, I'm sure you'd really like it.'

Five

Dominic's motor-bike was standing by a wall near the steps in front of the cathedral. It annoyed Karen that she had recognised it so easily. It must have been the fluffy thing, looking horribly like a rabbit's tail, that had caught her eye. It hung from one of the handlebars on a piece of red cord.

She was on her own, wandering round the city centre. Laura's symptoms had been the beginnings of chickenpox, and according to Karen's mother it could make you feel quite bad at that age. Now that the spots had come out she would probably be feeling better but Karen had decided to put off visiting her until the following day. When she did see her she was not sure how much she would tell her. Laura already disapproved of the way Karen had encouraged Hannah to talk about her family. Besides, there was absolutely nothing in the way of hard evidence.

There was the whispering of course, but Hannah might be jumping to conclusions. The rest of the family could be discussing her father, Jonathan, and how he was going to manage now he was a single parent. But there were two things which convinced Karen that the Tremlett family had something to hide. Sara had lied about the man in the purple sports car and been pretty unpleasant at the time, and Mrs Tremlett still seemed set on stopping Karen talking to her granddaughter. Of course, it was possible that whatever it was they wanted kept secret had nothing to do with the accident in North Devon.

She had been thinking about Trevor Osborne's description of Hannah's mother. When people said someone was a 'wild one' they didn't usually mean it as a compliment. Who else had been swimming in the sea at the time of the accident?

She could hardly ask Hannah to go over the incident in detail. That left Fran, but it was unlikely she would be prepared to talk to someone she had only known such a short time. If she and Trevor had discussed Petra Tremlett's death Dominic could well have overheard what they were saying. He was a pain, but if there was any chance he could turn out to be useful . . .

She watched his motor-bike from a safe distance, not wanting to give him the pleasure of thinking she had any interest in him, but curious to know what he was doing in the city centre. It was midday and the sun was beating down on her head. Trevor had said she should wear a hat, and Alex had told her off for not wearing one and covering herself with protective cream, but since Alex had burned his back and her mother had been forced to smooth special soothing lotion on it, he was hardly the best person to pass on advice. Nothing more had been said about the job in Oxford and she certainly wasn't going to raise the subject. *Let Karen think about it for a bit.* She could hear her mother's quiet, determined voice. *You know Karen, flies off*

the handle, then she'll calm down and realise it's not
such a bad idea after all.

Two hands covered her eyes. She spun round, expecting to see someone from school, and found herself face to face with Dominic Osborne.

'D'you mind?' said Karen.

'Not in the least.' His hands had dropped to his sides. He was wearing dark glasses that made him look stupid, like the kind of pop star who goes about pretending he doesn't want to be recognised.

He took off the glasses and put them in the pocket of his shirt, which was unbuttoned, revealing his suntanned chest.

'Laura's got chickenpox,' said Karen.

'Oh, yes. What about it?'

'I just thought you might be interested.'

'Oh, I am. Hope she doesn't scratch the spots and leave scars on her beautiful face. Want a Coke?'

Karen hesitated. 'I was thinking I might have a coffee, only I can't stay long.'

'Me neither.' He pointed to the bike. 'Don't want to come back and find someone's nicked it.'

He chose the nearest place – an 'olde worlde' café that charged a fortune – and ordered two coffees. Then he asked Karen if she had seen Hannah again.

'Not since we helped clear up the centre.'

'Tails and Whiskers,' he said. 'I ask you, could anyone think up a sillier name.'

'Your father said they need money from the public to really get it going.'

'Well, I doubt if they'll get any more from that Leo.'

'Hannah's grandfather?'

'Oh, didn't you know?' Dominic grinned. 'He bought the place for Fran. Reckon he decided it was the best way out of a tricky situation. After my mum went off with the Italian it only took a few months for Dad and Fran to get together. Bit of a laugh really. Fran and the gardener.'

'Your father was the Tremletts' gardener?'

'Jobs round the house, a bit of work in the garden. Mad as hell they were, but what could they do? Sensible way out was to set Fran up with the Rescue Centre. After all, the alternative would be having her live with us in a council house.'

The coffee was placed unceremoniously on the table.

'So,' said Dominic, 'you're as curious as I am to know how a proficient swimmer like Petra could be swept out to sea.'

'What makes you think I'm curious?'

He smiled. 'Couldn't have been cramp. You must remember that warm spell.'

'I should think the water was still pretty cold.'

He shrugged. 'Maybe. Even so, if you'd met Jonathan Tremlett . . . He and Petra hated each other's guts. And Jonathan wasn't the only one who couldn't stand her.'

'You knew Hannah's mother quite well?'

'I wouldn't say that.' He grinned, showing off the white teeth that contrasted with the darkness of his skin. 'Only met her three or four times, but it's not that difficult to tell, is it? Or perhaps you've led too sheltered a life.'

'My parents are divorced,' she said, stung into retaliating to yet another of his patronising remarks. 'My mother lives with another bloke.'

'Really?' He stirred sugar into his coffee, slopping at least a quarter of it into the saucer. 'What's he like?'

'All right.' She had no intention of telling Dominic about Alex. 'What's your mother's name?'

'Why d'you want to know? Lorraine.'

'Has she married again?'

'Who knows?'

'You mean you never hear from her?'

He shook his head. 'Daresay she'll turn up one day. Anyway, who cares? If she did I wouldn't bother to give her the time of day.' He was blinking fast, trying to keep control of himself, but giving himself away. Karen was sorry she had asked about his mother. Just because he was a big show-off she had made the mistake of thinking he had no feelings at all.

'Sara Tremlett,' she said, changing the subject, 'how much d'you know about her?'

'Ah, Sara.' Dominic glanced at the people sitting at nearby tables, then dropped his voice. 'Kind of woman blokes always fall for, only I reckon she'd make your life hell.'

83

'What makes you say that?' The coffee was incredibly bitter and some of the grounds had floated up to the surface.

'You've seen her, haven't you?' He pushed his cup to one side and leaned his elbows on the table. 'Never think she and Fran were sisters, would you? Mind you, she'll be losing her looks in a year or two. Bet the thought of it scares the pants off her.'

'She lives in London, doesn't she?'

He nodded. 'Has some high-powered job, selecting people for top jobs. Head-hunting, they call it.'

'Has she got a boyfriend?'

He shrugged. 'All these questions! Fran says she's had dozens but they never move in with her. Likes to keep her independence. A bloke would clutter up her life, untidy her smart flat.'

'You've been there?' Karen leaned forward, so as not to miss a single word of what he was saying.

'Me? Do me a favour. Fran has. It's near Regent's Park, full of stuff Sara's brought back from business trips abroad. Not junk, really expensive things, only just lately she's been selling it all off, says she wants to live simply, have a place like the Japanese, just a bed, table and chair.'

He looked at his watch, then pushed back his chair and stood up. 'Better check the bike.'

'Yes.' Karen was disappointed. There was so much more she wanted to ask and she might never get another chance.

'I'll tell you one thing,' he said, searching in his pocket for some loose change, then dropping a handful of coins on the table, although she could tell it wasn't enough to pay for even one cup of coffee, 'if anyone threatened one of her family that Ginny Tremlett would react like a tiger with its cubs.'

Karen laughed.

'You don't believe me?' he said. 'Shows how much you know about Hannah's grandmother. Anyone who crossed her, I reckon they wouldn't stand a chance. All right then.' He lowered his long dark lashes and let his hand brush against hers. 'How's this for a piece of fascinating information. At the time of the so-called accident

Leo Tremlett was out in a boat, not far from where it happened. Oh, I'm not saying it was his idea, more likely to have been put up to it by his wife, wouldn't you say?' He grinned again, pushing back his hair, then picked up the red and blue crash helmet he had left on the floor beside his chair. 'She was murdered, I can tell you that much for certain. If you want some more detailed info you'll have to stop giving me all those snooty looks. Right, well, I'll see you when I see you. Bye for now.'

She had been thinking about Sara Tremlett selling off her prized possessions. Was it really because she wanted to lead a simpler life, or did she need the cash? If she did it must be a fairly large amount. If her job was high-powered that presumably meant well paid.

Perhaps she needed money to give to Hannah's father? Fran had mentioned how attached to her brother Sara had always been. Now he was in trouble, what were a few ornaments compared with the opportunity to help bail him out.

The flash of colour went past so fast that Karen only caught a glimpse, but how many people in the area owned a low-slung purple sports car with fancy brake lights? First the motor-bike, now a car she couldn't fail to recognise.

When she turned the corner she could see it parked on the waste ground that had been cleared to build a new supermarket. Approaching it slowly, she scanned the area for the man with slicked down hair, but unless he was hiding behind a lamppost he was nowhere in sight.

The car turned out to be older than she had expected, although you couldn't tell from the number plate. It was one that had been bought specially. There was only one number and the letters were REV. Karen walked all round it, taking in the fancy steering wheel and the newspaper on the passenger seat, something called the *Sporting Life*. She wondered how you stopped people stealing a car that had an open top. Surely anyone who knew how to start the engine without an ignition key could jump in and drive straight off.

'Want a ride?' The voice made a shudder run through her body.

Like the car, the man looked older close to, about forty-five, maybe a little more. His eyes were a very pale grey and his eyelids drooped at the corners. There were deep lines running between his nose and the corners of his mouth, and he had a cleft in his chin that he kept fingering as he watched her face.

'Sorry.' She took a step back but the man moved nearer. 'My father used to have a car like this. Only his was green.'

The man smiled. He didn't believe a word of it. 'Really? They were very popular at one time. Don't see too many about these days.'

'No, that's why I'm interested in them.' Surely he hadn't recognised her. The time she had seen him, with Sara Tremlett, he was far too preoccupied to take any notice of a girl with a dog.

'I see.' His voice was mocking. 'And their owners – you take an interest in them too?'

She edged away, but he moved closer again. 'Where's the dog? Looked as though it could do with a bit more exercise. Cruel to let them get overweight like that, need to be put on a low calorie diet.' He patted his flat stomach. 'Don't know about you, but I make sure I stay in good shape.'

Karen was trying to breathe more slowly. The fear that he knew about her connection with the Tremlett family was turning into anxiety that he was going to grab her and force her into the car.

'Right,' he said suddenly, his expression changing to match the coolness in his voice. 'I'll make a deal. You stop spying on Sara and we'll say no more about it.'

She opened her mouth to say she had no idea what he was talking about, then thought better of it. Sara must have spoken to him. If she pretended she had never seen the two of them together it would only make him more suspicious.

'If you mean Sara Tremlett,' she said, 'I've never spied on her and I can't see any reason why I'd want to. The fact that I just happened to be taking someone's dog for a walk . . .'

Just for a moment he looked as if he believed

89

her. Then he gave her what he probably thought was a seductive smile and took off his jacket, throwing it over one shoulder so as to make sure she noticed the expensive blue silk lining. Suddenly he started to laugh. 'Hey, I was only joking – about the spying business. Thing is,' he rubbed at a tiny mark on the car's purple paint-work, 'no-one knows about me and Sara, except you of course, and Sara wants to keep it that way, just for the time being.'

Karen sighed. 'Yes, well it's nothing to do with me.'

'Good girl, glad you've got the picture. Now,' he lowered his head to get a better look at her face, 'how about a spin on the bypass?'

'No, thanks.'

'Don't trust me?' He laughed again. 'Quite right too. Shouldn't have put temptation in your way.'

With a quick movement he pulled open the car door and climbed into the driving seat. 'No hard feelings then, glad you like the car. Oh, just one more thing, Karen. That is your name, isn't it? Nice name, used to have a girlfriend . . .

Well, we won't go into that now.'

He paused, trying to remember the one last thing. 'Ah, got it. Memory like a sieve. Starts to let you down when you're my age, not that I'm over the hill yet, plenty of mileage left, isn't that what they say?'

Karen managed a weak smile.

'That's better. Nice smile transforms you. Now, what was I saying? The Tremlett kid. She was in the sea at the time of the accident and I reckon she may have seen more than she's letting on. Anything she tells you – well, put it this way—' He started up the engine and started slowly reversing off the piece of uneven ground. 'She's a very special person, is Sara, loyal, devoted. I wouldn't want her worrying about another member of the family. No, that's something I wouldn't like at all.'

Six

The worst thing about it was the spots on her scalp. Laura wasn't feeling ill, just fed up that if she tried going out people would think she was still infectious. Besides, how could anyone go out in the street looking like that.

'Some people look like that all the time,' said Karen. 'I mean, they put on all that stuff that's advertised in magazines but mostly it doesn't do a scrap of good.'

'If they're really bad you can get a prescription from the doctor,' said Laura. 'Anyway, I've never had those kinds of spots. Kate did.'

'Your sister? Has she had the baby yet? It must be funny having a sister who's eight years older than you are.'

'Oh, it's a huge joke.'

Karen sighed. She had called round, intending to tell Laura about the man with the sports car. Now she wasn't sure it was such a good idea. If Laura's present mood was anything to go by she would tell her she was making something out of nothing. She had been seen watching a man talking to Sara Tremlett, then a few days later, been caught red-handed examining his car. Wouldn't anyone have been suspicious of her?

'Seen Dominic?' asked Laura, inspecting herself in the mirror, but not for some tiny imperfection, the way Tessie often did.

'Hardly at all.' For some reason Karen thought it best not to tell her about the café near the cathedral.

Laura still had her back turned. 'I wonder if Fran knew what he was like. Before she married his father, I mean.'

'Must have done, I should think. Hey, why didn't you tell me Trevor used to be the Tremletts' gardener?'

'Really? So that was what all the fuss was about. My grandmother's one of those ultra discreet types who never says anything interesting in case she's accused of being a gossip. As far as I can remember all she told me was that Mrs Tremlett's daughter had met up with a local man and wasn't it nice for her after all those years of remaining unmarried.'

'Local man? People say that when they mean someone's not the right social class. It makes me ill. Anyway, what's wrong with being unmarried?'

'Nothing, that's what my grandmother said, not me.'

'Sorry.' Karen wondered if chickenpox had a way of leaving people irritable, depressed. 'Listen.' She decided it might be a good idea after all to involve Laura in the mystery surrounding Petra Tremlett's death. 'You're a good swimmer, you've won medals and things.'

'Not too bad.' Laura sat on her bed, then flopped back on to her pillow. 'I prefer diving.'

'Yes, but you can swim ten times better than I can. Anyway, if you were swimming in the sea and you met quite a strong current you'd still be able to save yourself, wouldn't you?'

'Depends how strong. There's currents round

the Channel Islands that can overturn a boat.'

'Yes, but people don't swim there. I'm talking about somewhere like Devon or Cornwall.'

'People drown every year because they've swum out too far and can't get back.' She frowned. 'Oh, you're not still going on about Petra Tremlett. Isn't what happened bad enough without you putting all kinds of ideas into Hannah's head?'

But it was Hannah herself who had brought up the subject of her mother's death, and shown Karen the postcards and photographs.

'Forget it,' said Karen, moving towards the door. 'Anyway, you look all right to me. People have got better things to do than stare at old chickenpox scars.'

'They're not scars.'

'No. Well, I'll give you a call. Oh, and don't worry about Hannah, she's fine. There's a fox at the Rescue Centre that's expecting cubs. When they're born Fran's going to let us help with the feeding if the vixen's not strong enough to look after them all properly.' It was horrible to end with a sarcastic remark, but she couldn't stop herself. 'Actually, I doubt if Hannah's given her mother's death another thought.'

Hannah was in the small garden area, pulling up weeds and dropping them into a cardboard box. When she noticed Karen she looked as if she was seeing things, then she stood up, rubbing the earth off her hands.

'I didn't think you'd be coming.'

'Why not?'

Hannah stared at the ground. 'I heard Granny on the phone.'

'Oh, I see. How did you know she was talking to me?'

'I didn't at first, then she said how she didn't want you to think you had to let me tag along.'

Karen frowned. 'Not what she meant though, was it? Just a not very subtle way of telling me I'm a bad influence.'

'Bad influence? I don't understand.'

'Nor me, Hannah, but I'm here so what's the plan for today?'

Hannah moved her head in the direction of the house. 'Dominic's up in his room. Fran asked him to give her a hand with some rolls of chicken wire but he said he'd do it later. He's a pig.'

'Oh, I don't know. Maybe he had a rough time the last couple of years.'

'Yes, I s'pose.' Hannah obviously didn't like the idea of Karen defending Dominic. 'But he ought to be glad Fran lives with him and Trevor. I bet it was awful before.'

'When his mother was there?'

'What?' Hannah looked a little embarrassed. 'No, I meant after she left. I liked Lorraine, Mummy did too, only I don't think she and Trevor were very well suited.'

Karen picked up the box of weeds and started walking towards the pile of rubbish at the other end of the yard. 'Is there something the matter, Hannah? You look a bit . . . Has something happened?'

'I had another postcard from my father. Actually two came on the same day, one from Florence and one from Milan, only I think they'd been posted at different times.'

'Let's have a look.' She put down the box of weeds.

Hannah felt in her pocket. 'They never say much. There's not much room on the back of a card.'

'That's why people prefer them to letters,' said Karen, 'saves having to think of things to write.' She regretted her remark immediately. It made it sound as if Hannah's father didn't care, as if he found writing a proper letter too much trouble.

'You can read them if you like,' said Hannah.

Karen turned over the first card. It was written with the same green ink as before. *Here I am in Florence. Fascinating place, wish you could see the architecture. Weather's too hot. See you soon. Daddy.*

'At least he says he's going to see you soon.'

Hannah sighed. 'He always says that. Read the other one.'

The second card had a picture of a statue. It was the kind you can buy in an art gallery and it made Karen wonder if Jonathan Tremlett might not have gone abroad at all. He could have written all the postcards at once and given them to a friend to post. If you didn't want anyone to find out where you really were that would be quite a good way of convincing them you were travelling round Europe on a business trip. But if he wasn't in Italy, where was he?

Milan's an amazing place, she read. *Still very hot but I'm starting to adapt to the temperature. Hope you're keeping well. See you soon. Daddy.*

'Lorraine lives in Italy,' said Hannah.

'Dominic's mother.' Surely she wasn't suggesting there was something going on between her father and Lorraine Osborne.

'They hate her,' said Hannah, 'at least Granny does. I suppose they think if it hadn't been for her, Trevor and Fran would never have got married. I don't think Grandad minds so much.'

Karen was still thinking about the postcards. *See you soon.* Why couldn't he tell her when he was coming home? No matter how bad he felt, it was wrong to leave her with her grandparents for weeks on end.

'Does your father always use that particular pen?' she asked.

'I don't know.' Hannah turned over the box of weeds and kicked at the heap of rubbish. 'He's got one of those laptop computers so he never writes if he can help it. Anyway, he hates me. No, don't say it's not true.'

'Don't be silly.'

Hannah had never looked so miserable.

'Listen, what I meant, since I've never met your father what's the good of me trying to—'

'I know. You're the only person who doesn't keep telling me stupid lies. He's gone away because he can't stand the sight of me.'

'But I thought he was on a business trip.'

'That's what they said, but they've started whispering again. When I come into the room they stop talking, or suddenly say something silly, like about the weather.'

'Is Sara still there?'

Hannah looked puzzled. 'Sara? She only came down for two days. Would you like to see the baby hedgehog? Fran says it's an orphan. It's got prickles but they're quite soft. I suppose they'd have to be or they'd hurt the mother when they were being born.'

A blue car was coming up the lane. It was moving very slowly, swinging from side to side in an attempt to avoid the potholes.

'Oh no.' Hannah hung her head.

'Who is it?'

'Granny. She uses that car if she drives in the country. Grandad doesn't like mud on the BMW.'

'Perhaps she's come to see Fran.' Karen remembered the advice she had given Mrs Tremlett on the phone. *You should go up there yourself sometime. I'm sure you'd really like it.*

The car had reached the gate. Mrs Tremlett parked it on the grass and started picking her way across the deep ridges of earth. She was dressed in a green calf-length skirt and a white blouse. The white sandals had been replaced by heavy brown lace-ups. She was frowning, shading her eyes from the sun, then she saw Hannah and started hurrying towards them.

'Wonderful news, darling.'

Hannah's eyes opened wide. 'Is Daddy coming back?'

'No, not Daddy, although I'm sure he'll be here very soon. Meg, your friend from school, her mother rang and asked if you'd like to stay on their boat near Chichester. If the weather's right they might even cross the Channel to France.'

'No thanks.'

'Oh, don't be silly, Hannah, of course you ought to go. Where's Fran? She is here, isn't she?'

The questions were addressed to Hannah. Karen might as well not have existed. Mrs Tremlett was hurrying towards the house, calling Fran's name. When she reached the door to the kitchen she peered through the window, then glanced back at Hannah.

'Have you seen her, darling?'

Hannah shook her head. 'Trevor's in there.' She pointed to the shed he called his bolthole. 'He might know where she is.'

Ginny Tremlett hesitated, not sure what to do next. Surely speaking to Trevor wasn't such an ordeal? When he and Fran were married had she and Leo gone to the wedding, or had it taken place in a registry office, with none of the family present?

'I think Fran's in the field,' called Karen. 'I could have a look if you like, just over there beyond the barn.' She caught up with Mrs Tremlett, leaving Hannah still standing in the yard. 'Of course, she could have gone for a walk.'

'A walk? I thought she was always so desperately busy. Listen, Karen, since you're here I'd like you to tell Hannah what a good idea it would be if she spent some time with her friend.'

'That's up to Hannah.'

Just for a moment she thought Mrs Tremlett was going to lose her temper. But she had far too much self control.

'What's going to happen when it's time for Hannah to go back to school?' Karen said quickly. 'I think she's rather worried about it. I mean, if she knew what had been planned for her she'd probably feel a bit better and she might even agree to stay with her friend.'

Fran was coming across the field. She looked as if she thought she was hallucinating. 'Mother? It's not Dad?'

'Dad? What on earth are you talking about? I've come to talk to Hannah, she's been invited to stay with a friend.'

'Oh, yes.' Fran glanced at Karen. 'Which friend is that?'

'A girl called Meg, who goes to Hannah's school.'

'Her father's got a boat,' said Karen. 'It's moored near Chichester, but Hannah doesn't want to go.'

Mrs Tremlett ignored Karen's comment. 'I'm taking Hannah home with me, to get ready. I don't want any fuss about the fox or anything. Has it had its cubs yet?'

'Oh, Hannah told you about it. No, probably not until the end of the week.' Fran wiped her hands on the sides of her corduroy trousers. 'Since you're here perhaps you'd like to have a look round the place.'

'Another time. I've rather a lot to do.' Ginny Tremlett turned to make sure Hannah was still there, then strode across the yard and took hold of her by the arm.

Hannah made no protest, but as she was leaving she looked back at Karen and Fran and mouthed three words: I'm not going.

A few moments later the blue car was bumping down the lane.

Karen stayed on at the centre, helping Fran clean out the rabbit hutches. She wanted to spend some time with her. She might even mention her new theory about the postcards. The Angoras had been christened Simon and Garfunkel. The names were Fran's idea, she had some cassettes by them and she was always singing *Bridge Over Troubled Water* and something about the sound of silence.

'Hannah misses her father,' said Karen. 'You don't know when he's coming back, do you?'

'Jonathan? Haven't a clue, I'm afraid. If there was any news I'm sure my mother would have passed it on. I did ask if she'd heard anything, but she just said he was terribly busy.'

'Don't you think someone ought to tell Hannah when she'll be going back to London?'

'Of course someone should, you're absolutely right.' She picked up a rabbit and held it high in the air, like people sometimes do with babies. 'You are a fine fellow. I *think* this one's the male.' She put it back in the hutch, then returned to talking about Hannah's father. 'As far as Mother's concerned, if Jonathan does or doesn't do something there's always a perfectly good reason for it. In her eyes he can do no wrong.'

'Does he often go away on business?'

'Oh yes, there's nothing unusual about that. Hannah's fretting, is she? The trouble is, she's like my mother, keeps everything bottled up, puts on a brave face. Of course, Sara's the same, I'm the odd one out. Mother used to say I wore my heart on my sleeve. Stupid expression, don't you think?'

'My mother once said the same thing,' said Karen.

'Really? How many in your family?'

'Just me.'

'Lucky you. As I say, Jonathan's Mother's pride and joy. Brilliant at school, a double first at Oxford, followed by an invitation to work on a research project. Then he met Petra.'

'At Oxford?'

'Oh, she wasn't at the university. It was at a party or something. Of course Mother and Sara tried to stop them getting married.'

'Why?'

Fran hesitated. 'Well, partly because they thought it would interfere with his career, I suppose, and partly because he was only twenty-two.'

They left the shed and came out into brilliant sunshine. 'So Hannah's father had to give up the research project,' said Karen.

'Oh, no, he and Petra were given some kind of allowance. That's the trouble with having rich parents, they can always buy you off with bribes. Complete your higher degree or else.'

It didn't sound like much of a disadvantage. 'Perhaps they didn't like Petra, thought she wasn't good enough for him.'

Fran laughed. 'That the impression you've got of the Tremlett family? Well, I can't say I blame you. Petra was even younger than Jonathan, only nineteen as I recall. He fell hook, line and sinker, as they say, looked happier than I'd ever seen him before, but of course Mother and Sara still thought of him as a little boy.'

'What about your father?'

'Oh, I don't think he was too bothered. Sara's always been his favourite. Sara's the first born, and Jonathan was the longed-for son.' She gave a short, bitter laugh. 'Oh, take no notice, being the pig in the middle has its advantages. People don't expect so much, you can hide in the background.'

'Yes, I suppose that's right.' Except when you decide to marry the odd-job man.

Alex had been short-listed for the job in Oxford. Karen could tell as soon as she saw her mother's face.

'He's so thrilled. Oh, don't look like that, love.'

'I wasn't. What about your job at the gift shop?'

Her mother shrugged. 'I'll find something else. Go on a course, maybe, have a whole new career.'

'What as? A brain surgeon?'

'Oh, come on, you'll like Oxford. Masses of things going on, fast train to London. I know changing schools will be a bit of a bore but now there's a National Curriculum it's not as if you'd have to—'

'I'm not going, I told you.'

'But you have to, love.'

'You mean you'll literally drag me there? Then what? Lock me up?'

Her mother's jaw had clenched but she was

making a supreme effort to stay calm, to say the right thing. 'Yes, well don't let's talk about it now. Alex and I are going out for a meal, only the Italian place near the clock tower, but we'd love you to join us.'

'No, thanks, I'm not hungry. Listen, if you went away and left me with Dad . . . No, I'm not talking about Oxford. Just for a holiday, I mean, or to buy stuff for the shop.'

'We'd never do that, it's all delivered to us from a central warehouse.'

Karen sighed. 'I wish you'd listen. It's just something I was talking to Hannah about.'

'That poor little girl, I'm glad you and Laura are being kind to her. Sorry, what was it you were saying?'

'If you were away on holiday for quite a long time, would you send me postcards?'

'Yes, of course, and letters, and I'd phone every week, twice a week at least, to make sure everything was all right.'

'But if you'd gone abroad, to France or somewhere?'

'They have phones in France, love. I suppose

110

if it was Tibet or Outer Mongolia . . . Now, change your mind and come with us to the restaurant. You can have anything you like, that dish with Pacific prawns, and some of that fantastic ice cream, all pink and green and covered in nuts.'

Karen was thinking about Mr and Mrs Tremlett and how Fran had accused them of handing out bribes to make their children do what they wanted. Was it the same with their grandchildren, no, grandchild? Hannah was the only one they had so far, and it didn't look as if they were likely to acquire any more. Would Ginny Tremlett find a way of bribing Hannah to go to Chichester? It would have to be a large sum of money, or something else, like a promise to get in touch with her father. Only Karen had a feeling that could be difficult, if not impossible. It had even crossed her mind he might not be alive . . .

'All right,' she said, giving her mother her sweetest smile, 'I'll come if I must, but it doesn't mean I'm going to move to Oxford. So promise you won't mention it again, all right?'

Seven

Her father was out of the office so Karen was spending the morning answering the phone and sorting out the mess of papers that had accumulated ever since he had given her an enforced holiday. Later in the day – *around six o'clock if that's convenient* – she had an invitation to visit the Tremlett house.

The invitation had come from Mrs Tremlett, not Hannah, but at least Hannah had got her own way over the Chichester business. Fran said her mother had given in gracefully. Karen doubted if that was quite right. Knowing Ginny Tremlett, there was bound to have been a price to pay.

The phone started ringing. 'Cady's Detective

Agency.' Karen said the words now without even thinking, that was why the voice at the other end of the line was such a surprise. 'Alex?'

'Look, Karen, you'll think this a bit odd but – well, I never seem to catch you alone at home.'

'What d'you want?'

'Oh, come on, don't be like that. It's about this job I'm applying for. I didn't mention it last night, didn't want to spoil a nice evening out, but the thing is, if you really don't want to live in Oxford—'

'Oh, don't worry about me, Alex, I'll be fine. I told Mum I'd be moving in with Dad.'

Alex sighed. 'Yes, but that's not quite the point. Your mother – I mean, we both want you to live with us. Anyway, what did your father say?'

'When?'

'When you asked if you could share his flat?'

Karen had been afraid that would be the next question. 'Talk to you later,' she said quickly. 'Just seen someone coming up the steps.'

It was a lie. Even Alex would know that. And he would know she hadn't spoken to her father about her plan for him to take on the lease of the floor above so there was room for a larger office, and enough living space for the two of them.

Karen pushed the window up, to let in more air, then gazed down the street, fanning herself with the folder she had made for phone messages.

'What on earth are you doing?' Her father was approaching from the opposite direction. 'The sash cord's frayed, if you're not careful you'll get your head chopped off.'

She shrugged. Her father noticed and pulled a face. 'Now what's the matter? No, hang on, wait till I've come inside.'

When he entered the office she was ready. If she didn't speak now she never would. She would lose her nerve and it would be too late. Or her mother would say something to him and any chance she had would disappear.

'It's about Alex,' she said. 'No, don't interrupt, I mean Alex's new job.'

'He's heard already?'

'No, but he's bound to get it. Listen, you know the offices upstairs have been empty ever since that computer company moved out . . .'

'What about it?' But she could see from his face he had guessed what was coming next. 'Not a chance, Karen, with overheads like that I'd barely break even. Anyway, it won't be that bad. You can visit whenever you like, see your friends, give me a hand with this lot. Oh, come on, it's not my decision. You know me, if I had the space I'd be delighted, but there's more to it than that. Your mother wouldn't like it at all.'

'I don't see why. I'd have thought she and Alex would be glad to be shot of me.'

'Oh, don't talk such rubbish.' Her father studied the computer screen, then made a flattering remark about her ability to sort everything out so well.

'Thanks.' She pretended to be pleased, to have accepted his decision, come to terms with the possible move. But the fight wasn't over yet.

'Had a nice evening out with your new girlfriend?' she asked. She considered making a remark about being a bridesmaid at the wedding, but she had said something similar to her mother and Alex and it hadn't gone down too well.

'Very pleasant, thank you. And thanks for all this.' He pointed towards the computer.

'I expect you'll be getting married again. I suppose that's why you don't want to rent the first floor and turn it into a proper flat, instead of living in two horrible, poky rooms.'

He leaned against the wall and folded his arms. 'Give it a rest, Karen. Now, how about getting out in the sunshine and enjoying yourself.'

'I'm not five years old, Dad.'

'Really? You could have fooled me.'

Without the tea tent and stalls the Tremlett garden looked even more enormous. A lawn, mown in stripes like Wembley on Cup Final day, stretched into the distance, and beyond that she could see a row of weeping willows that must mark the edge of the riverbank. There was a smell of mown grass. Karen wondered if Hannah's grandfather had taken over the garden since Trevor left, or perhaps they had hired someone new. She could imagine Ginny Tremlett cutting a few flowers for the drawing-room, but not doing any of the heavy work. Still, she could be wrong

117

there. Mrs Tremlett was not particularly tall but, if the large number of shopping bags was anything to go by, she was stronger than she looked.

As she walked up the drive Karen hoped Hannah would come out to meet her or, if not, Silas, wagging his tail and pushing his wet nose into her hand, but there was no-one to be seen. The front door had a bell and a knocker. Karen rang the bell, heard it echoing inside the house, and waited, trying to work out what to say when Mrs Tremlett opened the door. What *could* she say? She had no intention of standing there as if she had been summoned by the headmistress. On the other hand, there was no point in being paranoid. If Ginny Tremlett had agreed that Hannah could stay on, instead of joining her friend on the boat, perhaps she had had a change of heart all round and wanted to make it up to Karen, apologise for all the veiled threats and funny looks.

The front door opened wide and an old man with grey hair and a pair of glasses perched on the end of his nose stepped forward, holding out his hand.

'Karen?'

'Yes.'

The two of them had never been introduced but she recognised Hannah's grandfather at once. He was exceptionally tall and looked exactly what he was: a retired doctor, a specialist in – what was it? – heart disease.

'Mrs Tremlett asked me to call round,' said Karen, and because she was determined not to appear intimidated her words came out sounding almost rude.

'Yes, that's right. My wife's out at present, she's taken Hannah to visit a distant relative who lives about thirty miles away. Do come in.'

Karen followed him into the tiled hallway. There was still no sign of Silas, but she thought she could hear a faint whining noise down the end of a passage leading to the back of the house.

Leo Tremlett took a few paces to the right, then held open a heavy oak door and stood back for Karen to pass. 'After you, my dear.'

The room was a study, larger than the sitting-room at her home, but probably quite small by Tremlett standards. There were bookshelves on three of the walls and some of the books were very large. A quick glance showed that they had been arranged in alphabetical order, by author, and everything else in the room looked equally well-ordered.

Most of the pictures on the wall seemed to be of people, in old-fashioned clothes, studying gruesome-looking instruments. In one a fat, red-faced man with a monocle was bending over an ashen-faced patient. Karen wondered if they were supposed to be funny.

Two armchairs faced each other, in a space in front of the window.

'Have a seat.' Mr Tremlett opened one of the drawers in his desk, took out a box of tissues, then lowered himself into one of the chairs and stretched out his long legs in their rough tweed trousers. 'Don't worry, it's an allergy, not an infection.' He dabbed at his nose, then put the tissue in his waistcoat pocket. 'Does she talk to you?'

'Sorry?'

'Hannah, does she talk to you?' He studied the nails on his left hand. It was a way of not looking her in the eye. 'What does she say?'

'Nothing much.' Karen was thinking fast. 'Mostly we talk about the animals – at the Rescue Centre. We both like animals.'

He smiled. 'None of my business, eh? I'm inclined to agree. The reason my wife asked you to call round . . . I wouldn't like you to view it as the Spanish Inquisition, she just wants to help, you know.'

Karen made no comment. If Mrs Tremlett wanted to help Hannah she had a strange way of going about it. She had summoned Karen to the house, then gone out taking Hannah with her, and left her husband to do the dirty work.

Leo Tremlett took another tissue from the box and screwed it up into a ball in his hand.

'Perhaps we've been going about it the wrong way,' he said. 'Is that what you think?'

'I don't really know what you mean, only I think Hannah just wants to be treated normally, like before.'

'Before her mother's death, you mean. Yes, well, I suppose you could be right, but things have changed. It's not the same as before.'

Karen was starting to relax. She liked him better than Ginny Tremlett, he was warmer, less aloof, but, on second thoughts it could be an act, a bedside manner he had perfected over more than fifty years.

'No, but Hannah's the same person,' she said softly.

'Of course. Seems to have taken a liking to you, am I right? But since the two of you met, if anything we've been even more worried about her.' He saw Karen's expression and started to apologise. 'I'm sorry, that didn't come out at all the way I meant it to. It's just – well, her grandmother feels so responsible, and with Jonathan up in . . .' He broke off abruptly. 'I mean, away on business . . .'

'You don't know when he's coming back?'

He shook his head slowly. He was looking through the window, raising himself off his chair, as if he was expecting someone. Or perhaps he had noticed something strange outside. 'Hannah's very quiet with us. She was never one for chattering on, but from what I've heard she's opened up to you.'

122

'I don't know.' Suddenly Karen felt in control of the situation, rather than under attack. What could the Tremletts do to her? Ginny Tremlett had instructed her husband to pump her for information, find out if Hannah had told her something they ought to know. Something they wanted kept quiet?

'She misses her father,' she said. 'He sends her postcards but he never says when he's coming back.'

'She's shown you the cards? But she hasn't said anything else – about her father, I mean?' Leo Tremlett gave her a reassuring look, designed to convince her she could trust him. 'And her mother, poor Petra . . . Has she told you much about the accident?'

'Not really.'

'Tragic business. One wonders if anything . . . but in fact there was nothing that anyone could have done, absolutely nothing, it was just a freak wave that—'

'I thought it was the current.' The words had just slipped out. Karen regretted them at once.

'Both,' he said, watching her face intently, then

blowing his nose and dropping the tissue in a leather wastepaper bin. 'It's a dangerous piece of coast.'

Karen took a risk. 'Don't they have red flags to tell you when you're not supposed to swim?'

'Of course, but only on the larger beaches.' His piercing eyes meant she had to struggle not to look away. 'This was a small cove. As far as I can tell no-one's ever got into difficulties there before. Petra swam out too far, over-estimated her stamina. Terrible, none of us will ever forget. As I say, the only comfort's in knowing everyone did absolutely everything they could.'

Karen remembered Dominic mentioning how Leo Tremlett had been out in a boat. She longed to ask exactly what had happened, where he had been at the time, if he'd tried to reach Petra but been unable to get there until it was too late. Couldn't he have pulled her out of the water and tried artificial respiration?

'You think I'm prying,' he said. 'You dislike talking about Hannah behind her back, but you can believe me when I say we're only concerned with Hannah's well-being.'

You can believe me. Karen's eyes moved round the room, taking in the photographs on a table over by the window. Hannah when she was two or three years younger. Hannah with a man with wiry brown hair and glasses.

'My son,' said Leo Tremlett. 'Hannah's father.'

Karen stood up to have a better look. She made a few comments about family likenesses, but all the time she was checking to see if there was a picture of Petra. Sara's portrait had been taken in a studio – she looked like an actress or a fashion model – and there was another that must be her and Fran when they were in their early twenties. There was no photo of Fran's wedding; in fact, someone who knew nothing about the family would have assumed she was unmarried, that Trevor didn't exist. And not a single picture of Petra.

Leo Tremlett moved his feet impatiently. Karen returned to her armchair and sat waiting for the next question.

'The thing is,' he said, 'Ginny, my wife; she hates any unpleasantness, can't bear to see people suffering. Oh, not just the family. She's very well liked in this part of the town, always willing to give a hand, take over if someone's unwell, hold the fort if they have to go into hospital.'

Karen said nothing. What was she supposed to say? Leo cleared his throat noisily, then managed to regain his composure. 'Anyway, it was good of you to agree to come and see us.'

'That's all right.' She wanted to say she found it a little odd to be invited by Mrs Tremlett, then find she wasn't even there, but there was no point in increasing their hostility towards her.

'Oh, just before you go,' he said, 'my wife wondered if Hannah had been having bad dreams, nightmares?'

'If so, she hasn't mentioned it.'

'No?' His eyes were very still, unblinking. 'We were afraid she might be suffering post-traumatic symptoms. People relive the terrible experience and—'

'Yes, I know what it means. Why don't you ask her?'

Leo frowned. 'Oh, we've done that all right, but it occurs to me that she may find it easier talking to someone nearer her own age.'

He stood up, flinching a little, as if his knee might be giving him pain. 'If she did say anything . . . anything at all – about what happened in the sea . . .'

Karen stared at him, but said nothing. Their eyes met for an uncomfortable moment, then he looked away and moved towards the window. 'Oh, look, there's Sara, my daughter. She's been overdoing things a bit, needed a bit of a break. Went back to London after the weekend, then decided she needed to come back here for a while to recharge her batteries.'

Karen joined him and they stood together, watching Sara crossing the lawn with a large wicker basket in her hand.

'Loves gardening,' said Leo. 'Even managed to make something of the tiny space behind her flat. I gather the two of you met briefly, at the shopping centre. Come along and get introduced properly. Which school are you at? What are your favourite subjects? Sara's one of those people who does well, whatever she turns her hand to. She considered medical training, then decided against it and did a degree in psychology.'

They were walking back through the hallway. 'Yes, I heard she had a high-powered job.'

'Really? Who told you that?'

'It could have been Fran, or even Dominic. I forget.'

'So you're acquainted with the whole family.' Suddenly his voice had an unpleasant edge to it. 'Well, of course you are, if you're a regular visitor to the Rescue Centre. Tails and Whiskers, what d'you think of that for a name? Sounds like a children's picture book, but then Fran was always the sentimental type.'

And Sara's the wonder girl. Karen smiled to herself. She had a sudden vision of a board attached to the gate at the end of the drive leading up to the Tremlett house. It had a picture of some ferrets, or maybe a polecat with a bird in its mouth. The black letters, on a scarlet background, read Tooth and Claw.

Eight

The most recent card from Hannah's father was postmarked Napoli. Karen knocked on the door of the small stone building where Trevor kept his tools, but there was no reply.

'He might be in the field,' said Hannah. 'Fran said he was going to put up some stronger fencing where the goats pushed it down.'

Karen turned the door handle and it came open. 'I just wanted to look at a map of Europe. Last time we were in here I was looking at all his books about motor racing and I noticed he had quite a collection of maps.'

'I'm sure he wouldn't mind,' said Hannah, but she was looking round anxiously to see if anyone was watching them. 'Perhaps we should ask Fran.'

The shed smelled of wood shavings and tobacco. Karen had never seen Trevor smoking but perhaps he had a quick puff when nobody was looking.

'Over there,' she said. 'Look, most of the maps are Ordnance Survey ones, but this atlas looks the kind of thing we need.' She placed the heavy book on a rough wooden table and started turning the pages fast. 'Scandinavia and the Baltic. Central Europe. Iberian Peninsula. Italy!'

Hannah moved closer and started tracing the coastline with her finger. 'Lorraine lives by the sea – well, she used to anyway. I think it's somewhere near a place called Salerno.'

'And Salerno's near Naples.'

'Where Daddy posted the card.'

'Doesn't mean a thing,' said Karen. 'Look, I know it's not up to me to tell you, but I wouldn't mention any of this to your grandparents. They'd only start worrying about you. I mean, even more than they do already.'

What Karen really meant was that the Tremletts would be down on her like a ton of bricks if they thought she was putting fresh ideas into Hannah's head.

'Oh, I never tell them anything.' Hannah's expression was so serious, so intense, that Karen wanted to laugh. 'If they ask I just say I helped with the animals. Anyway, Sara's there at the moment and she looks so thin and ill, so they've forgotten about me, thank goodness.'

'What's the matter with her?'

Hannah shrugged. 'She's been overworking. She has to choose people for important jobs. Grandad says it's very stressful. They do interviews and give questionnaires and things.'

'Assessing people like inanimate objects. I expect she does that with her boyfriends too. Points for hair, teeth, height, weight and how much money they earn.'

'Why d'you say that?' said Hannah, frowning. 'I like Sara.'

'Sorry,' said Karen, 'I'm sure she's really nice. I don't know her at all, or your grandfather.'

She felt a little guilty, not telling Hannah how she had been summoned to talk to her grandfather. She had waited for Hannah to

131

mention it herself, then realised no-one had told her. Perhaps it was best to say nothing. It would only make her ask endless questions.

Since the visit to the Tremlett house Karen had been doubly certain the family had something to hide. Back home she had made a list of all the possible reasons why anyone would have wanted to get rid of Hannah's mother.

Her father, Jonathan Tremlett, was the obvious choice. He was missing, 'away on business' so everyone said, but Karen doubted if this was true. Had Petra, who Trevor had described as 'wild', driven Jonathan to such extremes that he was prepared to kill?

Then there was Mrs Tremlett who, according to Fran, would have done anything to guarantee her son's happiness. Had she and Leo planned Petra's death, fixing up the swim so that she was bound to get into difficulties? At first sight this seemed improbable – supposing Hannah had been caught in the current – but Leo had been ready in his boat if things failed to go according to plan. Of course, it was possible the whole family were in on it, even Fran, who Karen had grown to like a lot. Or she and Sara might have planned the 'accident' together. Fran, 'the pig in the middle', felt hard done by and took it out on the extrovert, fun-loving Petra, who should have supported her when she married Trevor but instead had sided with the family, treating Trevor as 'beneath contempt'.

Hannah was still studying the map, oblivious to the thoughts that had been going through Karen's head. She looked so thin, but there was something tough about her too. However much her grandparents wanted her to put the tragedy out of her head, there was no way she was going to stop speculating, not until she was absolutely certain her mother's death had been an accident. And definitely not until her father returned from the mysterious business trip nobody seemed to want to discuss.

'Come on.' Karen gave Hannah a push towards the door of the hut. 'Time to concentrate on the animals, help Fran and Trevor with whatever jobs need doing.'

'Yes, all right, but we're not allowed to go near the fox. Fran's worried she's becoming too tame.'

'Yes, I know, Fran told me.'

'What?' Hannah had caught sight of her reflection in the dusty glass and was examining it, twisting from side to side. 'I hate my hair,' she said suddenly. 'I wish I was blonde, like Mummy, or really dark like Dominic. Actually I'd like to look like Sara, wouldn't you?'

'Not particularly.' Karen felt hot and irritable, and just for a moment Hannah had reminded her of Tessie.

Hannah glanced at her, nervously. 'We could look at the owl, only I suppose she might get too tame as well.'

'Oh, don't be ridiculous. It's usually half asleep during the day so it's not even going to notice us gawping at it.'

'No, I suppose not. I was thinking, Karen, you know all those books Trevor's got about cars?'

'What about them?'

'Mummy was interested in motor racing. She used to go to Brands Hatch. Not with Daddy. I think she went with a friend.'

'You don't mean Trevor?'

Hannah looked at Karen as if she was mad.

'They couldn't stand each other. No, there was this man she knew. His wife had gone to school with Mummy or something. Anyway, he was mad on cars.'

'Did she tell you his name?'

'Yes, but . . .' She screwed up her face, trying to remember. 'Murray, yes that's what she used to call him, like the mints. And it wasn't his wife she knew, she'd met him when she bought a writing-desk from his antique shop.'

'Where was his shop?'

'Um, I'm not sure. She loved buying antiques. Daddy said it was costing him a small fortune. I think Murray's shop was in . . . Does it matter? If it does I'll try and remember. I could ask Sara, she likes old furniture.'

'No, don't do that, only if the name of the place comes back to you perhaps you could let me know.'

'Yes, I will.' Hannah looked at her curiously. 'Dominic says he's certain Mummy was murdered. Is that what you think?'

Karen felt a wave of sympathy. 'I don't know, Hannah. Maybe after something terrible happens

135

people find it hard to talk openly so everything seems more mysterious than it really is.'

'You don't mean that, I know you don't.' Hannah sat down heavily on a rickety chair and burst into tears.

Fran insisted on driving Hannah home. Had there been a phone call from the Tremlett house? Her bike was put in the back of the Volvo and she climbed reluctantly into the passenger seat, looking back over her shoulder at Karen, who was helping Trevor to fix a stable door.

After the others had gone the place seemed very quiet. Apart from Trevor's whistling all she could hear was the odd, low-pitched clucking of the chickens, their feathery legs like flared trousers.

'Buff Cochins,' said Trevor. 'Half a dozen Rhode Island reds would have done but Fran's got this thing about rare breeds.' He looked up at the sky and pointed to a heron flying overhead. So far he had spoken very little, but he was the kind of person you could be with, without feeling you had to break the silence.

His beard had been trimmed and it made him look less like one of the Seven Dwarfs; not that he was all that small, but he seemed quite old and he yawned a great deal, like Sleepy, and had a habit of whistling through his teeth.

He gestured to Karen to let go of the stable door, then swung it, testing the hinges for strength, and pronounced himself satisfied with the result.

'Like to see my office?' He had a screw in his mouth and for a moment she thought she had misheard.

'Yes. Thanks.' She had a twinge of guilt, remembering how she and Hannah had studied the map of Italy while Trevor was in the field. He was smiling to himself. Was he teasing her? Had he seen the two of them coming out of the shed?

'In here,' he said, pushing open the creaky door. 'Have to get away from everyone now and again, know what I mean?'

She nodded. By everyone, did he mean Fran and Dominic, or was he getting a bit fed up with the way she and Hannah kept visiting the place?

He began unwinding a bandage on his thumb. 'Hit it with a mallet, can't get more careless than that.' He held out his hand and she could see the blackened nail and the place beside it where the skin had been broken but was now starting to heal.

Out in the open she had enjoyed his company, enjoyed being able to learn a bit of carpentry, but here in his bolthole she felt slightly uneasy.

'Hannah had a postcard from her father,' she said.

'Oh, yes, did it say when he was coming back?'

'No. He's in Italy. The card had a picture of a square in Naples.' She watched him carefully but he seemed to be thinking about something else.

'So you never met Petra?' he said.

'I hadn't met any of the Tremletts until a couple of weeks ago.'

'Is that right? Should have hit it off, me and Petra. Of course she and Lorraine were thick as thieves. The three of us had something in common, see.' He laughed, then put his injured thumb in his mouth and gave it a suck. 'Outsiders, not quite up to the mark, not quite what Ginny had in mind for her precious offspring. What really got me at the time was that none of them seemed bothered about Fran's happiness, just how it would look to everyone else.'

'Some people are like that.' Karen wanted to hear more. 'Hannah was telling me how her mother was interested in antiques, used to go to a particular shop. You don't know where it was, I suppose?'

He looked at her curiously. 'Round here, was it? More likely to be in London, I'd have thought.'

'Yes, I expect so. The only reason I was interested, if it is near here, is that my mother runs this gift shop, mostly stuff imported from abroad, but they're thinking of selling old stuff too.'

It was a lie, not that Trevor was likely to have visited the shop.

'Bought things all over the place,' he said. 'Wanted her house to look like a showpiece, or so Lorraine used to say. Had a whole load of friends, didn't like being on her own, couldn't stand her own company.' He glanced at an old station clock attached to the wall.

'I'd better be going,' said Karen. 'I promised Fran I'd make a start on that long grass behind the barn. Thanks for letting me help with the stables.'

He nodded, then started opening and closing drawers. As she was leaving his head came round the door.

'Ask Dominic,' he said, 'if you really want to know more about Petra Tremlett. Regular little snooper he used to be. More interested in his bike now, but still, you never know.'

By the time Fran returned it was nearly six. Karen was surprised to see she had Sara with her. They gave Karen a wave, then the two of them continued on into the house.

Karen decided she had outstayed her welcome. She put away the shears that needed sharpening and had made blisters between her thumbs and index fingers, then collected her bike from behind the house.

On her way out she passed the kitchen window. It was half open and one of the curtains had blown through it and wrapped itself against the glass. Inside she could hear Fran and Sara talking in hushed voices, then all of a sudden much more loudly.

'But why?' Fran sounded outraged.

'I've told you, it's the only way. If he thinks there's more I haven't a hope.'

'So you haven't really given up altogether?'

'The flat's gone, lease had run out. I didn't bother to renew it. Anyway, how could I?'

'And your job?'

Standing perfectly still, hoping the bush with its mass of white flowers would conceal her if anyone happened to be passing by, Karen listened for Sara's reply, but it never came.

There was silence and Karen guessed Sara must either have shaken her head or shrugged. Then a chair scraped on the stone floor, and someone ran water into a kettle.

'She deserved it,' said Fran angrily. 'Yes, she did, you know she did.'

'No, you can't say that.' Sara's voice sounded shaky. Another chair scraped and Karen thought she recognised the sound of someone kicking a cupboard door. 'Don't! You'll break it. You'll hurt yourself. Please, Fran, what's the point?'

So Fran, who always seemed so calm, so gentle with the animals, so tolerant and good-natured, had another side to her.

When the noise subsided Karen could hear Fran crying. 'What about Jonathan, then? He'll never be able to stand it, not a tough regime like that. He should have gone somewhere quite different. It isn't fair!'

A door opened, probably the door to Trevor's shed. Karen crept from behind the bushes and walked quickly towards the gate, pushing her bike and humming cheerfully, just in case anyone suspected she had overheard the conversation in the kitchen. When she was a safe distance away she would start trying to work out what it had been about. *If he thinks there's more I haven't a hope.* More what? Sara must be referring to money. Was someone blackmailing her? And if so who was it and what did the blackmailer know that Sara was so desperate to keep a secret?

Dominic was coming up the lane on his motor-bike. When he reached Karen he pretended he was going to run into her, then came to a sudden stop, but left the engine running.

He was wearing track-suit bottoms and a black T-shirt with white writing, most of which had come off in the wash. 'Looking for me?' he asked.

'No.'

'Pity. I've got something to tell you.'

She hesitated, remembering how Trevor had described him as a snooper. 'Actually, there was something I wanted to ask you.'

He moved his eyebrows up and down, like a character in an old silent film. 'Sounds interesting. Not here though, the place might be bugged. Tomorrow, ten-thirty, that veggie caff in South Street. No, too early, not usually up by then, make it eleven-fifteen.'

Nine

Dominic was late. Well, what did she expect?
When he turned up at nearly half past he had an
expression of mock remorse.

'Sorry, trouble with the bike. No, not true.
Couldn't drag myself out of bed.' He pushed his
dark, shiny hair behind his ears. 'What're you
having? Oh, you've got something already. Think
I'll order a pizza.' He glanced at his watch. 'Be
lunch-time soon, besides I missed my breakfast.'

When he sat down his chair was much too close
to hers. She moved away and he laughed. 'Right
then, what is it you wanted to know? If it's about
Sara Tremlett I'm afraid I'll have to disappoint
you. Told you all there is. She's down here again,
don't ask me why, been talking to Fran, seems

to have lost some of her icy cool.'

Karen sipped the dregs of her cold coffee. 'You said you had something to tell me.'

'Did I? Memory like a sieve. Maybe it'll come back to me when I've had something to eat.'

Karen refused to rise to the bait. 'One thing I was wondering,' she said, 'what's going to happen to Hannah when the school term starts?'

'Search me. If Jonathan's not back I suppose she'll have to go to a school down here.'

'Have you ever been to the house in London?'

'Jonathan's place? Why would I have done that?'

'I just wondered. Your father said Petra collected antiques and the house was like a showplace.'

He looked at her curiously. 'You've been talking to my father? Don't tell me, you gave him a good grilling, then he passed you on to me, told you what a nasty little eavesdropper I was. That's the beauty of people treating you as if you didn't exist; nobody notices what you're doing and how many stray remarks you've stored away for a later date.'

'I thought you might know of a particular shop Petra visited.'

'And if I did?'

'Oh, nothing, it doesn't matter.' She finished her coffee just as Dominic's pizza arrived.

'Want some?' He cut a slice, dropping slices of green pepper and black olives on the table, then held it out to her, balanced on his knife. She shook her head. 'Oh, well, suit yourself. Since you're so interested in the Tremlett family I'll let you in on something that'll make your hair curl. Fran was talking to my dad a couple of days ago and I heard them mention Wandsworth.'

'What about it?'

'Not the area of London, idiot, the prison. "It's a tough one, Wandsworth," that's what my dad said, then Fran started sniffing.'

'You really think he's in prison?' Karen remembered the conversation she had overheard. Fran and Sara, in Fran's kitchen. What was it Fran had said? *He'll never be able to stand it, not a tough regime like that.* 'But surely they wouldn't be able to keep that from Hannah?'

He answered with his mouth still full of pizza.

'Don't see why not. It's trials that get heavy reporting. People on remand are just left to rot. Imagine old Jonathan, stuck in a cell with some hardened case who's seen it all before. Soft as butter, he is, be done over in no time, reckon he's probably in the hospital wing by now.'

'It's not like that if you're only on remand.'

'Want to bet? Incidentally, if you're really that interested in Petra I seem to remember her rabbiting on about an antique shop about twenty miles from here. Actually, at one time she visited the place several times a week. Hang on.' He took a ballpoint from his inside pocket, scribbled something on the back of an old lottery ticket and gave it to her. 'Anyway, if you're thinking of visiting the place I could give you a lift on my bike.'

'No, thanks, I just wanted the name for my mother.'

'A likely story. Hey, there *was* something else I meant to tell you. That Leo, he's not as old as he looks.'

'What about it?'

'A few months after he retired he suddenly

started looking about ten years older. That's what happens if you give up your job. Of course it all happened rather quickly, some indiscretion at the hospital, something to do with drugs I'd say, only I never managed to get hold of the whole story.'

Karen was trying to concentrate on what he was saying. It was too interesting to stop listening, but half her mind was on the name of the shop he had written on the scrap of paper. Not the name, that wasn't important. What had caught her attention was the colour of the ink in Dominic's ballpoint. It was bright green.

'So,' he said, 'have I earned another ten minutes of your company? Buy you another coffee?'

Karen looked up and saw Laura approaching from farther down the street. Since she was a vegetarian it was likely she frequented the café they were sitting in. At the very least she would probably look through the window in case someone she knew was inside. When she noticed the two of them it would lead to all kinds of questions. Why had Karen lied to her? Why was she with Dominic when, every time they met, she couldn't wait to tell her how much she disliked him? Explaining that she needed to find out more about the Tremletts would only make matters worse. *Oh, for heavens sake, you're not still stirring up trouble. I wished I'd never introduced you to Hannah. I might have known it would do more harm than good.*

'There's Laura,' said Karen. 'Look, I have to go, but I'm sure she'd be thrilled to see you.'

'Really? She's fit to be seen, is she? Spots have disappeared?' He stood up, pushing his plate aside, and accompanied Karen out into the street. 'Laura, how are you?'

He had done it on purpose. Karen was sure of that.

'Just been having an early lunch with Karen.' He put on his crash helmet and threw his jacket over his shoulder. 'Now you're better you must come round to the Rescue Centre again. All kinds of things have been going on, you'll hardly recognise the place.'

Karen was trying to think of a way of contacting

Hannah – to ask her what her mother's friend looked like, the one who had accompanied her to motor racing events, the one called Murray.

She could visit the centre but the chances were Mrs Tremlett had found a way of filling up Hannah's time with visits to relatives or theme parks, or the zoo in a nearby town. In the end she decided to phone. There was a good chance Sara might answer. She was unlikely to recognise Karen's voice and would think it was one of Hannah's friends from school.

Ginny Tremlett answered the call. She sounded hoarse, as if she had a sore throat, and she recognised Karen's voice at once.

'You want to speak to Hannah? She's out in the garden, I'll just go and fetch her.'

Well, it could have been worse. She waited for what seemed a long time, then Hannah came on the line, although Karen had a feeling Mrs Tremlett was still in the room.

'Hannah? Listen, it's Karen. Are you on your own? I wanted to ask you something but it may not be convenient.'

'Oh. Hang on.' Karen heard someone speaking

and then the sound of a door closing. 'Sorry. Granny was arranging some flowers. I told her I couldn't hear properly. What's happened? Have you found out something? I had another card from Daddy with a picture of the Eiffel Tower.'

'Really? He certainly seems to get around. No, it's about that man you mentioned, someone your mother knew called Murray, I think you said.'

'What about him? Why d'you want to know? It wasn't anything important, she knew lots of people.'

'Yes, I'm sure, but can you remember what he looked like?'

'I never saw him. He came to the house once, but I heard Mummy say she was rather busy and it wasn't convenient to invite him in.'

'Anything else?'

'She thought I couldn't hear. "Oh, Murray, what on earth are you doing here?" That's what she said. "I told you never to come here in the school holidays."'

'Go on.'

'No, there isn't any more. I think he was quite

old, but wore quite flashy clothes. Oh, and he probably had fair hair.'

'Why d'you say that?'

'I heard Mummy talking about him on the phone. "You know me, I prefer them dark, but there is something rather attractive about him."'

'Thanks.' Karen took a deep breath. 'Look, I'll see you soon. Tomorrow, up at the centre? If your grandmother asks why I phoned tell her I was passing on some news about the fox.'

'Is it all right?'

'Yes, as far as I know.'

'I could say you were worried about me because you hadn't seen me for a few days. Granny said I was looking peaky and ought to stay at home for a bit, only it's not true—' She broke off. Had her grandmother come back into the room?

'All right,' said Karen, 'don't worry. Bye for now and I'll see you very soon.'

The coach took less than an hour, but that was the easy part. Karen had looked up the antique shop in the phone book and discovered the name of the street, but she had no map so she had no idea if it was in the centre of town or out in the suburbs.

She asked the woman in the ticket-office at the bus station but she wasn't much help. 'Couldn't say, love. I should turn right at the end there.' She pointed towards the window. 'Then right again and straight on towards the town centre. Someone there will be able to give you directions.'

'Thanks.' But supposing the antique shop was in some out-of-the-way place?

She thought about buying a map, but it was such a waste of money just for looking up one street called Bloxham Place. A group of French students had blocked the pavement and two people who looked like teachers were trying to make themselves heard above the noise. Karen waited impatiently, then squeezed past, glancing up a side road in case it had the name she was looking for, but it was called St Anne's Way and led up to a park with tall iron gates.

When she reached the usual row of chain stores it occurred to her that it would be quite possible to look up the street without actually buying a map. Choosing a crowded gift shop, its windows crammed with outsize teddy bears, she pushed her way to the back, found what she wanted and managed to read the index without doing any harm to the map. Bloxham Place. When she unfolded the right section she could see that it was only a short distance away, but the network of small streets made it quite difficult to memorise the route.

Left, then left again. She crossed a square, where most of the houses had been converted into offices for solicitors or accountants, then turned down a narrow street with a row of shops that all seemed to sell junk or antiques. Some were fairly up-market, others had the kind of stuff most people would have disposed of at their local refuse dump. Karen almost tripped over the handle of an old lawnmower and a woman rushed out to see what the noise was about, muttered something inaudible, then waddled back inside the shop.

The next shop had started life as a small gallery, but now sold plant pots and ceramic figures. Karen studied Dominic's piece of paper but there was no place of that name. A man was trying to start a car. When he climbed out and opened the bonnet Karen approached him, holding out the paper, and asked if he could help.

'Standing right in front of it, love.' He pointed to a shop with its windows boarded up and a To Let sign stuck on the door. 'Went out of business, oh, must have been four or five months ago.'

'Did you know the person who owned it?'

The man straightened up. 'Why d'you want to know?'

Karen thought fast. 'He's a friend.'

The man looked her up and down. 'I'll believe you, thousands wouldn't. With friends like that . . . If you want my opinion I'd stay well clear.'

'Yes. Thanks.' She stood there for a moment, wondering where to go next. The man had his head under the bonnet of his car again, but she could feel him watching her out of the corner of his eye. She decided to return to the safety of the main street with its familiar chain stores and crowds of jostling shoppers.

So her journey had been a waste of time.

Glancing at her watch, she was surprised to discover it was already nearly five. The coach had been late arriving. No wonder she felt starving hungry. A Mars bar would do, but as she turned the corner she thought she could see a place that sold sandwiches. It was down a short road that had been pedestrianised. Beyond the sandwich bar was a florist's and beyond that a pub called The Bearded Goat that had five or six tables set out in front of it.

She walked quickly into the sandwich bar and ordered half a baguette with egg mayonnaise. While she waited she looked through the window, watching a cat that had climbed into a flower-bed newly planted out with pink Busy Lizzies. It picked its way between the flowers, then settled down on a warm slab of stone in the centre.

Two women came out of The Bearded Goat, then a man carrying a tray of food. Karen's heart started thudding and she turned quickly away, concentrating on the shelf behind the counter, staring at the cans of Coke. A large woman, dressed in a white silk jacket, was following the man. She had their drinks in her hands, and she was squeezing between the tables, holding the glasses high in the air. She was wearing very high heels and seemed to be having difficulty keeping her balance. Each time she spilled the drinks she started to laugh so that even more slopped onto the ground.

The man's suit had been exchanged for jeans and a suede bomber jacket but she would have recognised the slicked back hair a mile away, and since he was in the same town as the now defunct antique shop, there was little doubt in her mind that Sara's friend and the man called Murray were one and the same person.

He found a table and the two of them sat down. From the way the woman was looking about her Karen had a feeling she had never visited the town before. She removed her silk jacket, revealing a bright pink shirt, then draped the jacket over the back of her seat. Next she searched in her bag until she had found a small mirror, which she held in front of her face as her other hand applied more lipstick. All the time she was talking non-stop, jerking her head in the direction of the old buildings on the other side of the street, then at a tall church spire in the distance. Suddenly she dropped the lipstick into her bag and leaned across the table. As she was planting a kiss on his mouth the man looked up, and the soppy expression that had been on his face a moment before changed to one of surprise, then cold anger.

He had seen Karen, their eyes had met, and he had realised she was checking up on him. As she left the sandwich bar a voice yelled, 'Hey, your egg mayonnaise.' She started to run.

Ten

The end of the pedestrianised area had been cordoned off and beyond the red and white barriers men with pneumatic drills were digging up the tarmac. Karen looked wildly round, searching for a shop where she could go in one entrance and come out of another. But it wasn't that kind of an arcade.

ARNFIELD CARPARK – LOWER GROUND ENTRANCE said the sign. In a multistorey carpark there would be any number of places she could hide. Ignoring the lift, she ran up the first flight of steps, glanced through a gap at the top to make sure she could still see the tables outside the pub, then climbed to the third floor and positioned herself between a camper van and a white Mercedes.

She guessed the woman was in her late forties, about the same age as the man she now called Murray. It was impossible to hear what she was saying, of course, but she didn't look English, not because of her coarse dark hair or the way her skin was so deeply tanned, but because of the way she was using her hands as she talked.

Murray had placed a green cardboard box on the table. He pushed it towards her and she opened it with enormous care and lifted out something wrapped in tissue paper, a china figure that could have been a dog, or perhaps a lion. Murray smiled, then took the figure from her hand and turned it over to show her the maker's mark on the base.

Karen felt dizzy and realised she had been holding her breath. Leaning against the side of the camper van she started to plan how to leave the carpark and make her way back to the bus station. Murray would have seen her enter the swing-door – there was little doubt in her mind about that – but he would have no idea which exit she was going to take. All his attention was on the china figure, but a moment later she saw him lean across the table, kiss the woman lightly on the cheek, then start walking away in the direction of the boarded-up shop.

Weaving her way between parked cars, Karen reached the stairs and ran down them until she reached what she hoped was street level. The place seemed to have been built on a slope and a floor that was underground at one entrance was on the ground floor at another. The doors opened automatically as she walked towards them and came out at what looked like the back of the shopping arcade. She glanced quickly round, afraid that Murray might have made an inspired guess and be waiting a few metres away.

There was no-one in sight. Breathing more easily, she set off towards the tall office building that she knew was quite close to the bus station. Murray had no means of knowing how she had come to the town. She could have caught the train, or been given a lift by her parents or a friend. He couldn't be in more than one place at once so the chances of him finding her were virtually nil.

She was walking fast, away from the town

centre, but being careful to choose a route that would lead eventually to the bus station, but from a different direction. The office block was a hideous building that towered above everything else, but it made a useful landmark. When she found her way back she would hide across the other side of the road, wait until the coach was just about to leave, then jump on at the last minute. If he ran after her she would scream and he would be too afraid to catch hold of her in broad daylight, with people watching.

Fifteen minutes later she reached what looked like a ring road. There was grass on either side, then a narrow pavement, then houses set well back, with large front gardens. The clouds had dispersed and she felt hot and sticky, and very hungry. Leaving the sandwich bar without the baguette had been a mistake, but she hadn't been thinking straight then. She had panicked, assumed the man called Murray was out to get her, when more than likely he was just playing his usual game, trying to scare her, then making out it was all some kind of joke. Cars whizzed by, only a few metres away. A light aircraft flew overhead and Karen remembered how Alex had once said he was going to give up working at the Arts Centre, get a pilot's licence and make a fortune taking aerial photographs of people's country estates. She hadn't bothered to ask about the job in Oxford, but presumably it was at another arty place, where people sat around eating carrot cake and wholemeal scones before they watched some boring foreign film.

It all happened so quickly. One minute she was gazing up at the sky and the next someone had grabbed hold of her wrist and was pulling her into a car.

'No.' She shouted as loud as she could but the sound of the traffic was much louder. Her legs were being dragged clear of the door and an arm had reached across slamming it shut. A moment later the purple sports car surged forwards, swinging into the right hand lane, then roaring towards a roundabout, where it took the second exit and sped off towards the motorway.

'So,' said Murray, 'you couldn't leave well alone.'

'I don't know what you mean.' But even as

she spoke she realised how ridiculous she sounded.

'Come here often, do you?' His speech was slurred and she could smell the alcohol on his breath. 'Thought I hadn't spotted you? Nothing wrong with my eyesight, nothing a good pair of contact lenses can't cure. And the cunning little escape into the multistorey carpark. D'you know, you actually had me fooled for a moment, then I positioned Eva near one exit and kept an eye on the other two myself.'

'Why did you follow me?'

He laughed. '*Me* following *you*? I rather thought it was the other way round. Hey, do up your seat belt, we don't want to pull up with a jolt and watch you crashing through the windscreen.'

She fumbled with the buckle. Murray leaned across to help, his arm brushing against her cheek. 'Murray Fuller,' he said. 'And you're Karen. Karen Cady, whose father runs a detective agency. See how well briefed I am, although I can't imagine why you came looking for me. The shop was it, you wanted to buy some antiques?

And who was it told you I had a shop?'

She said nothing, but he gave her a dig with his elbow. 'Come on, we might as well be honest with each other. I like a good showdown, don't you?'

'I forget. Dominic, I think.'

'Dominic, the wayward stepson? I've never had the pleasure, but Sara's told me all about him. Friend of yours, is he?'

As he joined the motorway a driver hooted loudly. Murray looked over his shoulder, shouting abuse, then swung wildly from lane to lane. 'Come on then, what is it you want to know? No, I mean it, I've nothing to hide, it's just that I'm not too fond of being followed about by a schoolkid.'

She was frightened, but not so much of Murray as of the way he was driving. He was drunk, hardly capable of walking straight by the look of him, let alone being in charge of a powerful sports car.

'I wanted to help Hannah,' she said. 'No-one ever tells her anything so of course she imagines the worst.'

'The worst being what?' He sounded more amused than annoyed.

'That her mother's death could have been avoided in some way.'

He laughed. 'But that would have meant Hannah drowned. Or do you mean she suspects foul play?'

Suddenly he was overcome by a violent fit of coughing. For a moment Karen was afraid he was going to be sick, then he gained control of himself and started winding down the window. The noise of the traffic made it hard to hear what he said next. She had to lean towards him so that the sour smell of alcohol was even worse.

'Am I to take it that Hannah believes someone had a reason to do away with her mother? D'you know, I think she could be right. What a woman, should never have married Jonathan, fell for the whole idea of being part of an upper class set like the Tremletts. Well, it can't have been Jonathan himself, can it? Hardly her type, that's why . . . latched on to . . . on to . . . latched on to me.'

He could hardly get a whole sentence out

without jumbling the words, but having started the story he seemed unwilling to stop. 'Someone who could handle . . . make feel secure. Know what I mean or haven't . . . haven't a clue.'

Drops of rain had landed on the windscreen but he hadn't bothered to turn on the wipers. 'Going to live together,' he said. 'Petra. Lovely Petra . . . and Hannah . . . of course Hannah. Great plans. New life in Australia. New Zealand. She'd have . . . Hannah, she'd have . . . got used to me in no time.' The car almost touched the barrier on the central reservation, but he just managed to get it back on to the road. 'Hannah, I'm talking about . . . your friend Hannah.' He swerved to avoid a coach and the second near miss seemed to sober him up a little.

'Don't know about you,' he said slowly, trying to control his words, 'but I always think it's better to tell kids what's going to happen after . . . after all the details have been worked out. Know what I mean? Saves a lot of . . . saves a lot of heartache. Wouldn't you agree?'

They were going south. It was the first time Karen had managed to spot a sign. He was taking her back to her home town. He wasn't going to hurt her, just give her a fright.

'Well, look at it this way,' he said, winding up the window again and losing his grip on the steering wheel so that they almost bumped against another car. 'If the family hadn't found out about me and Petra she'd be alive today. Not that Hannah's grandparents ever knew a thing. If they've any suspicions now they're of their own making. But Fran and Sara . . . Ah, Fran and Sara, that's a very different matter.'

Finding out the direction they were travelling had given her courage, but she had to fight to stop her teeth chattering. 'Could you slow down a bit,' she asked. 'We're going to have an accident.'

'Whatever you say, Karen. Open the glove compartment, there's a flask wrapped in a . . . wrapped in a yellow duster.'

She hesitated, then did as she was told, and passed him the flask. He unscrewed it with one hand, took several swigs, then started talking in an almost normal voice. 'Hair of the dog, Karen, works like a dream.'

She stared through her window, trying to focus

170

on the distant hills with their tops covered in cloud. In spite of her fear she had to find out more. 'Anyway,' she said, her voice sounding unnaturally loud, 'if it's true what you've told me – about you and Hannah's mother – you don't seem very upset about her death.'

'Oh, I was upset all right, upset and extremely angry. Trouble was, Karen, who was going to believe me? Who was going to believe what I'd seen with my own eyes? Standing on the cliff-top. Not just any old binoculars, Karen, these ones are high-definition.' He twisted round, as if he thought the binoculars might be on the back seat, and the car lurched to the left, then back into the fast lane.

Murray drew in breath sharply, then turned to smile at her. 'No-one to corrob . . . corroborate the evidence. Old Leo out in his boat, pretending to fish, Fran sitting on the rocks in that terrible swimming costume of hers – and the rest of them in the water.'

'You mean Hannah and—'

'—Jonathan and Petra. Oh, and Sara, of course, don't forget Sara. People said there must have

been a freak wave, but if there was I never saw
it.'

They were overtaking a Range Rover, pulling
a large boat on a trailer. As they came within
centimetres of the boat Karen closed her eyes
and hung on to the sides of her seat.

'Petra had swum out quite a way,' said Murray,
'and Hannah was on her way to join her. Then
all of a sudden she was calling out.'

'Petra was?'

'Cramp, I suppose, or perhaps there really was
a current running. Jonathan grabbed hold of
Hannah, and Sara swam towards Petra. Sara's a
good swimmer, ask anyone, but you'd have
thought she'd never been in the water before.
Petra was drifting out to sea, her head
disappearing below the surface, then rising, then
gone again, then . . . Finally, with Sara still twenty
or thirty metres away she went down for the last
time.'

Sheep were grazing in a field, just next to the
edge of the motorway. They must have been
shorn. It made them look absurdly bony and
unsheeplike. So Sara, who could have saved her

sister-in-law, had allowed her to drown. A choice of evils. Which was worse: to kill her in a moment of anger, or to watch in cold blood as her lungs filled with salty water and she floated, face down, dragged by the current away from the shore?

'How do I know you're telling the truth?' she asked.

Murray cleared his throat noisily. 'Why would I make it up?'

'I don't know, there could be lots of reasons.'

'Sara knew it was true, otherwise she wouldn't have been paying out all that lovely cash.'

So, she had been right when she suspected Sara had been selling off her treasured possessions to raise money, rather than because she had decided on a change of lifestyle. When the money ran out she had been unable to renew the lease on her flat. But what about her job? Perhaps she had thought if she had no money there was nothing Murray could do to her, short of going to the police. But he was right when he said it was unlikely anyone would believe his story, so why had Sara agreed to pay the money in the first place?

'If she hadn't paid up I'd have told her parents,' he said, taking another large swig from the flask. 'They could never be certain I was telling the truth but it would have preyed on their minds till their dying day. The reason I was visiting the town, that time you saw me down by the river, and the other time when I caught you giving the car the once over – Sorry.' He broke off, having lost the thread of what he was saying.

'You were telling me why you'd visited the town.'

'Was I? Oh, that's right. Just to let Sara know she couldn't escape that easily, that wherever she went I'd still be around.'

He switched on the car radio and the two of them listened to the last few words of an old Elvis Presley song: *It's now or never, come hold me tight, kiss me, my darling, be mine tonight.*

'Elvis,' said Murray, turning up the volume. *Tomorrow will be too late. It's now or never, my love won't wait.* 'Now, in case you're thinking of making even more trouble, you'd be wasting your time. I'm leaving the country, going to where I can soak up the sun all year round. Me and Eva. Eva and me.'

'The woman outside the pub?'

'Rolling in it, she is, and can't get enough of me. Who could ask for anything more?'

Why had he told her all this? But she knew why. He was drunk, people who drank heavily always talked too much, they couldn't stop themselves. And he prided himself on living dangerously. He was even more of a show-off than Dominic, poor old Dominic whom she now suspected knew nothing about what had happened to Petra Tremlett, and had just made up a few stories to get her attention.

'Now, hang on to your hat,' said Murray, changing down a gear, then accelerating so that the car, which was already going fast, suddenly leapt forwards, 'and I'll show you what this monster was built for. Flat out for the next few miles, police willing, then I'll drop you off within easy walking distance. How's that for a generous offer?'

Eleven

Maybe it was some kind of a joke, dropping her off within two hundred metres of the Tremlett house. She felt sick and dizzy, partly from lack of food and partly from the journey down the motorway. During the last part, when Murray had shown her 'what the monster was built for', she had been convinced she was going to die. The wrecked car would be found, together with her body and Murray's, and her parents would never understand where she had been. Would Sara Tremlett draw her own conclusions and provide a possible explanation? It seemed unlikely.

Just before they reached the final exit a car in front of them had slowed down as a van pulled out to overtake. Murray had slammed on the brakes and the sports car had skidded across three lanes, narrowly missing a petrol tanker.

Back on the ordinary road he had asked if she had enjoyed her trip. He wasn't joking – he was too far gone for that. Perhaps it had been coincidence that he had stopped so close to the Tremlett's house, or perhaps his booze-soaked brain had gone into automatic and he had driven there without any conscious thought.

Someone had left the gate open and Silas was sniffing in the long grass at the edge of the lane. Karen's legs felt weak, as if she had just stepped on to dry land after a long voyage in a boat. She took hold of Silas's collar and guided him back into the garden, closing the heavy gate behind her. It was nearly eight o'clock. She had noticed the large old-fashioned clock built into the sports car's dashboard, just a few minutes before he had pulled up, telling her to get out, think herself lucky and keep her mouth shut unless she wanted Hannah to suffer even more.

'Silas, silly old dog.' She patted his broad back in an attempt to start returning slowly to something approaching a normal state of mind and body.

Then she realised the garden was full of people. It was an illusion, nothing like the day of the garden party, the day Laura had first introduced her to the Tremlett family. Six or seven of them were having drinks on the lawn. Ginny Tremlett sat on a straight-backed canvas chair, like a queen on a throne, and on either side of her were her two daughters. There was no sign of Leo, but Hannah was sitting cross-legged on a rug that had been stretched out on the grass, and standing just behind her, with a wine glass in his hand, was a tall, thin man with wiry hair, whom Karen knew at once must be Hannah's father. A few metres away Trevor leaned against a tree, smoking a cigarette. Dominic had climbed on to a branch where he sat swinging his legs.

Hannah spotted her first.

'Karen!' She started running towards her, ignoring her grandmother's request to slow down or she would fall and hurt herself. 'He's back. Daddy's back.'

'That's good.' Karen's voice sounded shaky. She tried again. 'Good, I'm really pleased but I think I'd better go, you're busy.'

'No, please stay.' Hannah took hold of Karen's arm and started pulling her towards the family party.

'Karen, how nice.' For once Ginny Tremlett looked as if she actually meant it. 'Have some lemonade. Hannah, darling, could you find your friend a glass.'

'Thanks. I just came to tell Hannah about a moorhen I'd seen. Actually since you're here, Fran, I might as well tell you. It's down by the river and it's got what looks like fishing line wound round its leg. I wondered if someone—'

'RSPCA,' said Fran, 'they work with the National Rivers Authority. Let them know and they'll come in a van, see if there's anything they can do.'

'Yes. Right. Thanks.' No-one had bothered to introduce her to Jonathan, but he stepped forward to introduce himself.

'Jonathan Tremlett, Hannah's father. I've been away on business, got back to Heathrow this morning.'

'No wonder Hannah's looking so happy.' Karen found a vacant chair and sat down. Just for a moment she had been afraid she was going to faint.

'She seems very pleased to see you too.' Jonathan's face showed the strain he had been under for the past few months. Karen still had no idea where he had been. If the rest of the family, apart from Hannah, knew, Sara certainly hadn't passed on the information to Murray. Perhaps the cards had been genuine, posted during a business trip, and he had been too preoccupied to realise that Hannah might have wanted a proper letter.

Mrs Tremlett was wearing the flowered dress she had worn on the day of the garden party. Her best clothes to welcome her son home?

'You say you've seen a moorhen, Karen. That's not the same as a coot, is it? I'm not very well up on water birds.'

'No, moorhens are smaller with a red beak.' The conversation was crazy, like a dream. 'Coots' beaks are white.'

'Isn't that interesting.' Mrs Tremlett turned to

Fran. 'You must find it useful having Karen around at the Rescue Centre.'

Hannah had returned with a glass. She filled it with Coke, spilling a fair bit, just as she had that first time she and Karen had talked to each other in the kitchen.

Karen took a few sips, then stood up again. 'Sorry to be a nuisance, Hannah, but you promised to show me those photos you took at the centre.'

For a split second Hannah looked puzzled. 'Yes, of course, they're in my room.'

'Photographs, Hannah?' said her grandmother. 'You never told us. Have they come out well?'

When they reached the house Hannah let out a long sigh. 'I'm sorry. You look awful. Are you all right? Granny said everyone had to come round. I don't see why she couldn't have waited till tomorrow, Daddy's terribly tired. He ought to go to bed.'

'The family,' said Karen, 'it's something that means a lot to your grandmother.'

'Yes.' Hannah started up the stairs. 'Sometime

I'd like you to meet Daddy properly. He's not like the rest.'

The side door was pushed open and Dominic appeared in the hallway. 'What's going on, then? Any fool could tell there weren't any photographs, and as for the story about the moorhen— Thought it up on the spur of the moment, did you, Karen?'

Hannah stood for a moment, frowning, then ran up the stairs. 'I'll be down in a minute. As a matter of fact, I did take some photos. The fox has had her cubs, there's three of them and they're really sweet. Fran came and fetched me in the car.'

Dominic opened the door to Leo's study. 'Quick.' He pulled Karen inside, then started talking very fast. 'I'm not supposed to know and for heaven's sake don't tell Hannah, but Jonathan hasn't been abroad at all. He went funny in the head, had some kind of breakdown and crashed out with monks or Buddhists or something, in a remote part of the Scottish Highlands.'

'Who told you?'

'No-one. I heard Fran talking to my father. And

all those postcards Hannah got – written before Jonathan dropped out, then posted by a friend touring Europe. Look, can we meet up some time? I need to explain.'

'Explain what?' Her voice was colder than she had intended.

Dominic hung his head, in mock regret. 'I expect you realised I was only joking when I told you all that stuff. About Petra being murdered. And Jonathan being banged up in Wandsworth.'

She nodded. She was too tired to do anything else.

'I just thought a few stories would liven things up a bit,' he said. 'Encourage you to stay around the centre.' He pulled a silly face, hoping to persuade her to agree it was all a great joke, then when this failed he tried another tack. 'All right, don't say it. Yes, well I guess that's as near an apology as you'll get.'

Her head was buzzing. Sounds were distorted. The voices of people close seemed to be coming from a long way away. Hannah came downstairs with the photos and the three of them walked back across the lawn, with Dominic droning on about some problem with the kick-start on his bike, and Hannah handing her one photo after another and waiting eagerly for her response.

'Karen, you're not even looking at them. Are you sure you're all right?'

'Yes, I'm fine.' She was watching the back of Sara Tremlett's head. The long neck that looked even longer because of the shortness of her hair. The delicate silver chain round her neck. The leather bag, with all its zips and pockets, lying by her side on the grass.

What wouldn't she give to ask her about that day on the beach and how she had hated her sister-in-law so much she was prepared to let her drown. So that Hannah could stay with her father instead of being taken to Australia? For the sake of Mrs Tremlett, who would have lost her only grandchild? Or was it because she had hated Petra ever since Jonathan had brought her home to meet them all?

Murray would be on his way back to the woman called Eva, the one who had so easily replaced Petra Tremlett. Petra had been in her early thirties when she drowned. Eva was more than ten years older, but she had the advantage of being rich. In a few days time the two of them would be sitting in a bar in the French Riviera or the Costa del Sol. Murray would put away the money Sara had given him, and live off Eva, probably marry her. Then when he grew bored . . .

A car had turned into the side entrance. Karen looked over her shoulder and saw the tall figure of Leo Tremlett climb slowly out of his BMW, then start walking towards the group on the lawn. As he passed quite close by she could see how agitated he looked. He glanced at Hannah, then hurried on. A moment later she saw him dabbing at his nose with a tissue as he searched for the right words to tell them all what had happened.

'A sports car . . . crossed the central reservation . . . narrowly missed several other cars, then careered back the way it had come—' He was so out of breath he could hardly go on talking. 'Left the motorway and rolled down an embankment . . . police, fire engines, ambulance, but the driver never stood a chance.'

'How frightful.' Ginny Tremlett glanced at

Hannah, wondering if she ought to be protected from hearing about such things.

'That's why I'm so late,' said Leo. 'Had to give a statement to the police. Eye-witness account, although it was difficult to describe exactly what . . . All took place so fast . . . Just seemed to lose control completely.'

Karen was shaking so much she was sure someone would notice, but when she spoke her voice was amazingly steady. 'What colour was the sports car?'

Everyone turned to look at her. What a question. A man had been killed and she wanted to know the colour of his car.

'Oh, no trouble remembering that,' said Leo. 'It was purple, bright purple. Not a new model so I imagine it might have been resprayed.'

Sara rose from her deckchair, then bent down to pick up her bag. 'I've a bit of a headache,' she said quietly. 'I think I'll go indoors for a while.' She glanced at Karen, her face as expressionless as ever, but just before she turned away Karen noticed the smallest flicker of a smile. The nightmare was over and no-one, apart from her and Fran would ever know the truth.

Karen wanted to run after her and explain how Murray had told her everything. About the swimmers in the water and how he had watched the whole thing from the cliff-top, with the aid of his high-powered binoculars. But what good would it do? And there was Hannah to think about. She was watching Karen, anxiously. She knew something had happened, not just the accident with the purple sports car, but something much more frightening.

'Come on,' said Karen, 'let's have a look at the river. It is the river over there beyond those trees? And you can tell me about the fox cubs. What a swindle, you seeing them without me. I had to go somewhere this afternoon but tomorrow, when your father's feeling better, maybe we could all go up to the centre and show him round.'

Twelve

'Alex had his interview,' said Karen.

'Already? Did he get the job?'

'They gave it to a woman. Alex said it was positive discrimination; if he'd called himself Alexis and worn a bit of make-up he'd have been home and dry!'

Laura laughed. 'So you won't have to move.'

'Oh, I wouldn't have gone to Oxford, whatever.'

They were walking by the canal. Further back the water had been full of little kids in canoes, being instructed for the first time how to sit up straight and hold a paddle. Now everything was quiet, apart from the distant sounds of a cricket match across the other side of the water meadows.

'Well, what would you have done?' said Karen. 'No-one knows the truth, apart from Sara.'

'And you,' said Laura. 'And what about Fran and Hannah's father?'

'I doubt if either of them saw what really happened. Jonathan was too busy saving Hannah.'

'Fran knew about the blackmailing.'

'Yes, but I expect Sara told her Murray had made up lies and was threatening to upset the whole family. I thought Hannah's grandparents had something they wanted to hide, but that wasn't right. They didn't want Hannah to find out about her father having a breakdown. They had no idea about the drowning.'

Sara, her father's pride and joy. Karen remembered Leo Tremlett's words. *Sara's one of those people who does well, whatever she turns her hand to.*

'Petra was going to leave Jonathan,' she said. 'None of the family would have seen Hannah ever again.'

'No, that can't be true. Parents are allowed to see their children.'

'When the father's in England and the child's in Australia? So what would you have done?'

'Told the police? No, I can see there wouldn't have been much point in that. Even if they believed you there was no-one who would have supported your story, apart from this Murray person.'

'I didn't mean that,' said Karen slowly. 'I meant what would you have done if you'd been Sara Tremlett?'

Laura was outraged. 'However horrible Hannah's mother was that wasn't a good enough reason for letting her die.'

When Karen said nothing Laura continued angrily. 'Anyway, you should never have started asking questions, following people around. That Murray person . . . You might have been killed on the motorway.'

Karen shrugged. 'Once you start thinking about what *might* have happened . . . Hannah's mother might not have gone swimming.'

'I might not have persuaded you to go to the garden party. You might not have taken your neighbour's dog for a walk and seen Sara talking to Murray.'

They stood on the bridge, watching the shoals of tiny fish darting between the waterweeds.

'I'm sorry,' said Karen at last, 'I shouldn't have told you. Now we'll both have to lie awake at night thinking about Sara and how she's got away with it, and there's nothing anyone can do.'

'Yes, I know.' Laura's anger had disappeared, she just looked tired, almost as tired as Karen. 'But you had to tell someone. I'm glad it was me.'